Mrs Caldicot's

To Nancy

Vernon Coleman

and very best wishes from Vernon Coleman (and Thelma Caldicot!)

ISBN: 978 1 898146216

Dedication

To Antoinette as always. You are my heroine. I am addicted to you. My life is you.

Acknowledgement
My wife, Antoinette, not only persuaded me to turn my existing books into ebooks but also to create new ebooks. I was pretty well ready to retire, and the first two books about Mrs Caldicot would have disappeared completely – probably for ever. It is entirely through her encouragement, initiative, determination and understanding of a process which I find utterly incomprehensible that any of my ebooks exist. So, thank you, Antoinette.

Note
This is the third book about Mrs Caldicot.

In the first volume, *Mrs Caldicot's Cabbage War*, a recently widowed woman (called Mrs Caldicot) was put into a grotty nursing home by her greedy son and daughter-in-law. Rebelling at the rules and regulations (and the smell of cabbage) Mrs Caldicot walked out and was followed by the other residents. After some adventures (and unexpected publicity including a memorable interview on television) Mrs Caldicot opened her own old folks' home and welcomed all her companions as residents. (This book was filmed as *Mrs Caldicot's Cabbage War* – starring Pauline Collins as Mrs Caldicot, Peter Capaldi as her son and John Alderton as the nasty nursing home owner.)

In the second volume, *Mrs Caldicot's Knickerbocker Glory*, Mrs Caldicot (the OAP's champion) was living with the former residents of the Twilight Years Rest Home. She has to fight local bureaucracy and struggle to raise the money to keep her nursing home open. In the end, she found a happy (and very simple and logical) solution. The Twilight Years Rest Home became her home and the residents became her family. This was a good thing because I tend to like happy endings and would have been disappointed if the book had ended sadly. Finally, there was, of course, a romantic conclusion: Mrs Caldicot married Jenkins, the newspaper editor.

Mrs Caldicot's Oyster Parade is the third volume of Mrs Caldicot's adventures.

Chapter One

The Great Adventure, if that is not too grand a name to use to describe what was originally intended as nothing more dramatic or exceptional than a relatively short trip to Paris, had started a few weeks earlier.

It was a Saturday evening when the seed of the Great Adventure started to sprout.

The staff and residents of what had previously been the Twilight Years Rest Home (but which was now informally known, both to the residents and to the local tradespeople, as Caldicot House) had been gathered in the sitting room staring goggle eyed at the television set.

They were, it is fair to say, as excited as they had been since the accelerator on the mobility scooter got stuck and Mrs Torridge had to drive round and round in circles until the scooter's battery ran down.

And that, it has to be said, was a day to be remembered.

Mrs Torridge herself thought it was all great fun, especially since the other residents ran alongside and handed her bars of chocolate to keep up her strength. (Mrs Caldicot said she didn't think it would be a good idea to give her drinks, though she did not explain that her thinking behind this apparently heartless instruction was that Mrs Torridge was known to have a small bladder.)

Eventually the mobility scooter's battery gave up the ghost, as these things usually do, and, having coasted to a halt just a yard from the front door, Mrs Torridge clambered off, stretched her legs, rubbed her now stiffened arthritic knees and waved to the assembled spectators with aplomb, pride and pretence at self-effacing modesty. She could have been a racing driver pulling into the pits after a famous victory or, possibly, an astronaut just returned from an excursion to the moon.

But that was ten days before the evening when the Great Adventure began.

Mrs Caldicot and her friends were all gathered in the sitting room and it was generally agreed that, although nothing had yet happened, this was even more exciting than Mrs Torridge's caper with the mobility scooter.

Most of those present in Caldicot House were on tenterhooks. The remainder were best described as agog.

Dr Roget, the eminent, English medical man who gave us the thesaurus which bears his name, would have doubtless moved effortlessly into top gear and bandied around words such as: excited, impatient, keen, curious, expectant, longing, avid, breathless and phrases such as 'waiting with bated breath' and 'on the edge of their seats'.

But on tenterhooks and agog sufficed as choices for most of the residents, thank you very much, though Ruth, the 18-year-old assistant housekeeper and a girl who believed in grasping life with both hands, managed to be both on tenterhooks and agog.

Normally thought of as a calm, peaceful and apparently unflappable girl, Ruth had discovered depths of emotional turmoil she had never previously imagined. She had, for several days, been telling everyone who would listen to her that this was, without a doubt, the most exciting thing that had ever happened to her.

Mrs Roberts, the housekeeper, and as kindly a soul as you are likely to find outside a Home for Retired Saints, twice had to tell Ruth to close her eyes and to do some deep breathing exercises in order to calm herself down a little.

Ruth, who was without doubt an excitable girl, had been at the shops and had missed Mrs Torridge's adventure on the mobility scooter so the only other exciting thing that had happened to her in recent years had been the occasion when an unexpected gust of wind had blown several of Miss Nightingale's unmentionables off the washing line and into the upper branches of a large silver birch tree. The previously mentioned unmentionables had remained in situ for the best part of four days, out of reach even of Mr Livingstone when he stood on the top rung of the longest ladder they possessed. The unmentionables had hung around blowing in the wind and drawing admiring glances from many passers-by and an enquiry from the postman as to whether they were to be there permanently as part of some promotional campaign. Eventually, an exceptionally strong breeze had brought them down onto the shed roof from whence Mr Livingstone had been easily able to retrieve them.

Secretly, hidden deep within her heart, Ruth still regarded the time when Steven Longley had kissed her when they were both 12 as the very, most exciting thing that had happened to her. They had been playing postman's knock one Christmas. However, she wasn't about to mention that, ever, to anyone else. Steven was now going steady with Elsie Weatherall, who was widely suspected to be no better than people thought, and Ruth had long since abandoned any idea of a rerun of that distant but magical moment.

Apologies are due, for your historian has digressed.

The reader will doubtless want to know the reason for all this excitement.

The fact is that Thelma Caldicot, together with the staff and residents, who shared the home where she lived, were waiting for the results of the weekly lottery draw on the television.

Lest criticism be forthcoming from those who regard all games of chance as inherently sinful, it has to be pointed out that neither Mrs Caldicot nor her friends and colleagues could be described as inveterate gamblers. On the contrary, this was their first brave foray into the world of commercial chance.

For the nub of the tale is that they had purchased a lottery ticket and were now desperately waiting to see if they had won a prize.

They had entered this strangely invigorating world, after Mrs Caldicot had found a £2 coin on the front drive outside their home.

When Mrs Caldicot had failed to find the owner of the coin, it had been decided, by a simple voting system that would have been the envy of any democracy, that the money should be used for some communal purpose.

Furthermore, it was then decided that since you can't do much with £2 these days (most of the residents could remember when you could buy a week's groceries, half a dozen bottles of decent wine, a load of oak logs, an armful of books and a nice hat with silk flowers for £2 and still had enough change to pay the rent and buy a bag of coal but, sadly, inflation had done the job it does so well and those days were now nothing but fading, sepia memories) the coin should be used to purchase a lottery ticket.

Ruth had been dispatched to the local shops to make the investment and now the stake holders were sitting watching the television set and awaiting the results of their first foray into the world of organised gambling.

Miss Nightingale and Mrs Peterborough were particularly excited because they had convinced themselves that they were taking part in something which Mrs Peterborough insisted on referring to as 'the numbers racket'. If they won, they expected the booty to be brought round by a man in a black suit and a black homburg hat.

Miss Nightingale said she thought he would probably be carrying a violin case though when Mrs Peterborough questioned her about this, she had to admit that she had no idea why this should be. She said that perhaps gangsters were so keen on playing the violin that they took their instrument with them wherever they went.

The two of them were expecting a police raid at any moment and for them this added to the general feeling of excitement. Miss Nightingale was so excited that she went so far as to perform a simple plié, segueing into an arabesque and following that with a grand jete which neatly, and entirely accidentally, removed Mr Roxdale's cup from his saucer. Fortunately, the cup was nearly empty at the time and it flew through the air with little damage being done. The cup was caught by Mr Livingstone who held it up as though he'd taken a catch in a big match.

Mrs Caldicot couldn't help smiling.

Miss Nightingale had trained as a dancer and for three years had worked as a ballerina with the Royal Ballet. There had been talk of promotion and the magical words 'prima ballerina' had been whispered. Tragically, her career had come to a crushing halt after a motorcycle accident had left her with a badly broken femur which took years to mend properly. By the time she could walk again, her ballet career was merely a memory. Worse, far worse, was the fact that her fiancé had been on the front of the motorcycle and he had died in the crash. Miss Nightingale, who had trained as a school-teacher when her ballet days were over and who had spent most of her life working as a primary school headmistress, had only recently started to dance again.

Mrs Caldicot herself had the lottery ticket in her hand but Mrs Roberts had copied the six numbers which were on their ticket onto a piece of cardboard, and she had placed the cardboard above the television set. This simple device meant that as the television host read out the winning numbers, everyone in the room could follow their fortunes.

When the television announcer had finished reciting the winning numbers, Mrs Caldicot and her friends owned a ticket on which five of the six numbers which had been read out.

'How much is the first prize?' asked Mr Hewitt.

'I read that the big prize is £22 million this week,' replied Mrs Roberts.

'So we should get five sixths of £22 million!' said Mr Livingstone, who would have been jumping up and down with excitement if his arthritis hadn't been playing up.

'Five sixths of £22 million is £18.33 recurring million,' said Mr Twist, a human calculator who had, in what he now considered to be his misspent youth and middle years, been a tax inspector working for the Government.

Mr Twist now looked after the books for Mrs Caldicot and helped stave off such unwanted nonsenses as penury, bankruptcy and debt collectors. His knowledge of the vagaries and peccadillos of the staff employed by Her Majesty's Customs and Excise enabled him to ensure that Mrs Caldicot's finances remain as close to healthy and legal as is possible. Caldicot House (since that is how the residents and local trades people customarily refer to the house, it seems only polite to retain that name for this account) had ceased to be a nursing home or, indeed, anything else official, and was run as a private house with a good many permanent visitors – each paying whatever they could towards the upkeep of the house and the provision of meals and warmth. Those residents who could help in the running of the establishment did what they could.

Mr Twist attempted to temper the assembled company's enthusiasm by pointing out, in his own rather gloomy way, that three quarters of big lottery winners go bankrupt and end up with less money than they had before their big win.

However, to his surprise, this news was greeted with cheering. 'Rags to riches and back again!' cried Mr Livingstone. 'What an exciting roller coast ride!'

'Sensibly, I think we should remember…,' began Mrs Roberts very quietly. But no one seemed much interested in a sentence which began with the word 'sensibly'.

‘We’ll have to decide whether or not to go public with our win,’ said Ruth, with great seriousness. ‘It’s an important decision. If we say we want to go public we’ll probably have to be prepared to do interviews and go on television shows.’

Ruth was a big girl (she had weighed her age in stones since she was ten-years-old) but not a bright girl. She was, however, a kind girl and, as Mrs Caldicot said to Mr Jenkins when ruminating on which of the applicants to accept when she was looking for a new member of staff, ‘an ounce of kindness is worth more than a pound of brains when you’re looking after old people who aren’t always entirely sure who they are, where they are or why’.

‘I don’t think we need worry about any of that just yet,’ said Mrs Caldicot, who didn’t want everyone getting too excited. She still remembered her own rather traumatic experiences with television interviewers and didn’t fancy the idea of repeating them.

‘How much money is that for each of us?’ asked Ruth. ‘If we divide eighteen and a bit million between us?’

‘How many of us are there?’ asked Mr Twist, looking around to count the number of heads.

‘Fourteen,’ replied Mr Merivale, who after using up his own fingers and thumbs had co-opting some of his wife’s digits to make up for the shortfall. ‘Everyone here, plus Mr Jenkins, of course, because he’s as entitled to a share of the ticket as anyone else.’

Everyone agreed that Mr Jenkins, who was Mrs Caldicot’s husband and who lived with her in the flat upstairs, was definitely entitled to a share of the winnings since he, as a resident, was definitely entitled to a share of the £2 which had bought the ticket and, equally certainly, also entitled to a full share of any winnings which might accrue.

Mr Jenkins was, at that moment, shut in the spare bedroom which he used as a study, working on a novel he was writing. He had never written a novel before and he was currently on the 11th draft of page one. He insisted, however, that he was definitely making progress and had told Mrs Caldicot that he had high hopes that he would soon be able to start page two.

Jenkins had been inspired to write his novel after reading lines from a poem by Ralph Waldo Emerson, the American essayist and poet.

The poem was called Terminus and the inspirational phrase was: 'It is time to be old, to take in sail…'.

'I may be old,' said a defiant Jenkins when he had read these words, 'but old age is a time to take on new adventures, to try new paths. It is not a time to take in sail.'

(As another aside, and this will be the last unless there are more, it should, perhaps, be explained that Mrs Caldicot liked to be known as Mrs Jenkins in her private life but as far as the residents and staff were concerned, she was still Mrs Caldicot. When she had first tried to explain to the residents that she would henceforth be known as Mrs Jenkins, there were some tears from Miss Nightingale and Mrs Peterborough who thought that this meant that Mrs Caldicot was going to leave them and be replaced by a Mrs Jenkins.)

'So how much is that for each of us?' repeated Ruth, who was so excited that she could not sit still.

'It's over a million pounds each!' said Mr Hewitt.

Ruth, who was immediately dreaming of private aeroplanes, yachts, Italian villas and the lifestyles of the rich and famous, went bright red with excitement. It is fair to say that she was not totally averse to the prospect of becoming a millionairess. Mr Twist's gloomy prognostication of almost inevitable personal bankruptcy worried her not a jot. She had just £27.38 in her current account and if winning and spending a million pounds meant sacrificing her £27.38 in the process of becoming a millionairess, or as a consequence of becoming a millionairess, then it was a sacrifice she was quite prepared to make.

'Approximately one million three hundred thousand pounds each, I think you'll find,' said Mr Twist. He looked around at the assembly and then suddenly sensed their alarm at having in their midst someone who could do such unnatural things with numbers without using a calculator or even having access to a piece of paper and a pencil. 'Just over a million and a quarter each,' he said, quietly correcting himself.

Ruth, eyes closed and dreaming of a world in which mops, buckets and dishwashers had no place, now added a French gigolo and a tattoo on some private part of her person to her wish list of a private aeroplane, a yacht and at least one Italian villa. The tattoo would, she thought, have to be somewhere not quite so private that no one could see it and that she couldn't show it to good friends, such as the French gigolo, if the occasion warranted it.

'I don't think it works quite like that,' said Mrs Roberts, louder now. She didn't want anyone to think of her as what her mother would have called a wet blanket but who nevertheless felt that someone ought to keep a finger hold on reality, and was the only person in the room who had studied the rules.

They all looked at her.

'I'm afraid we won't win all that much,' she explained gently. 'There will probably be a lot of people with five correct numbers. Only people who have all six numbers win the really big prizes.'

'So, how much will we win?' asked Mrs Merivale whose financial ambitions were modest but who thought she would perhaps use her winnings to treat herself to one of those tummy tucks she had read about in her favourite magazine. It would, she thought, be more painless than another attempt at dieting.

'I don't know,' said Mrs Roberts. 'We'll have to wait and see when the lottery people publish the details of what the prizes are going to be.'

And so everyone except Ruth had to put their dreams back into their boxes, close the lids for a while and wait.

Ruth's dreams were perhaps of sterner stuff. Or maybe she had simply not heard Mrs Roberts's warning remarks. Whatever the cause, she was still wondering what her French gigolo's attitude towards tattoos would be. Might he find a tattoo rather downmarket? It would have to be very tasteful. She somehow knew that you wouldn't see millionairesses wandering around Monaco with great big snakes curling round their arms or with bunches of roses adorning their breasts. If they had a tattoo it would be something small and very tasteful; something discreet. She thought of vulgar Sandra Pettigrew, who was three months into having a hunt in full cry tattooed on her back, with the plan being to have only the fox's tail visible at the very bottom of the spine, and she shuddered with embarrassment at the very thought.

No, she thought, a tasteful flower on a hip, would be appropriate.

Chapter Two

It was Monday before they heard the lottery results and discovered the extent of their riches.

They had won £2,892.

It wasn't just over a million, just under a million or anywhere near a million. But it wasn't a kick in the teeth either. And by the time they got the results, the expectations of the residents and staff had largely diminished, thanks to a large dose of communal realism setting in.

The communal realism had been aided and abetted by the strong feeling that winning over a million pounds wasn't the sort of thing that happened to real people who inhabited the real world. And there had also been a sneaky subconscious feeling that winning that much probably wouldn't be a good idea anyway. The truth was that they were all pretty happy with their lives and didn't want everything to be changed by having to find somewhere to park a fleet of Rolls Royces and private helicopters.

And so it is undoubtedly true that the residents and staff were probably more excited by this modest win than they would have been by a more momentous triumph. This was real money which could be spent on something that they could understand and enjoy.

'How much is that each?' asked Mr Hewitt.

'It's a little over £200 each,' replied Mr Twist, who had learned his lesson and was content to think with precision but articulate in more rounded numbers.

'Very nice too,' said Mrs Merivale. She didn't really want a tummy tuck, anyway. She hated needles and Mr Merivale always said he liked her just the way she was. 'Don't you go all skinny on me,' he told her when she had talked of going on a diet. 'If I'd wanted a skinny wife I'd have married a broom handle.'

'It would be nice if we could spend it on something we could all share,' said Mr Livingstone.

This was greeted with a considerable amount of wise nodding and it was generally agreed that this would be much more fun than spending the money individually. No one had thought of putting their winnings aside. What is the point of saving a £200 windfall? Even Ruth, her dreams put safely back into their box, thought that a communal spend would be more fun. The tattooist who had the studio over the launderette had charged more than £200 to tattoo 'Mum' and a small bunch of flowers on Eric Parton's triceps. Somehow, the tattoo no longer seemed a worthwhile expenditure.

'So what shall we buy?' asked Mrs Torridge.

'Could we buy a big box of chocolates?' asked Miss Nightingale. She thought for a moment and then added: 'But not too many of the sticky, chewy ones.'

'Not the sticky, chewy ones,' agreed her friend, Mrs Peterborough with a shake of her head. 'They get stuck in my teeth.'

There was then a lively discussion about how their unexpected winnings could best be spent. Some of the suggestions were sensible. Some were not so sensible.

Mention was made of a second mobility scooter (the residents who needed help in getting about shared the one which Mrs Torridge had driven round and round in circles) but this attracted little enthusiasm since the residents rarely had any great desire to travel around the neighbourhood.

There were mutterings about a new dartboard (quickly squashed by Mrs Caldicot who had hidden the only flight of darts after an unfortunate and entirely accidental incident involving Mr Hewitt's right arm and Miss Nightingale's left buttock) and some talk about investing in a greenhouse (supported with some enthusiasm by Mr Hewitt and Mr Roxdale but no one else).

Mr Twist suggested that the money should be put into a savings account for emergencies (this was pooh-poohed on the grounds that it was a boring thing to do with an unexpected windfall and partly on the grounds that it would not be enough to enable them to deal with a serious emergency).

Mr Williams suggested that they should blow the whole lot on a slap up meal at a local restaurant.

Mr Livingstone said it would be good to buy a new trumpet since they didn't have a single trumpet in the house. But even Mr Livingstone had to admit that this was not really in the spirit of the sense of togetherness and camaraderie that they were hoping to cement with their winnings.

'We could go to Paris together,' said Mrs Roberts, suddenly.

Everyone looked at her.

'For a little holiday,' explained Mrs Roberts. 'We could go over just for a few days. Since we won the money together it would be nice if we could spend it doing something together.'

And suddenly, it was generally agreed that a trip to Paris would very much fit everyone's bill. Those, like Mr Williams, who had been to Paris before thought they would very much like to see it again. And those who had never been were keen to see it for the first time.

Ruth, who, in view of the reduced size of their win, had now completely forgotten her dreams of gigolos, Italian villas and private aeroplanes, saw herself vaguely and ineffectually resisting the enthusiastic and amorous advances of a dozen over-romantic Frenchmen, all sporting waxed moustaches, wearing berets and carrying armfuls of red roses. None of them wore tattoos, as far as she could see.

'Is there enough money for a trip to Paris?' asked Mrs Caldicot, who had always wanted to go to Paris but who was rather doubtful that £2,892 was sufficient to pay for fourteen people to go to Paris, stay in a hotel and, most important of all, come back without having to swim across the Channel on the return journey.

'Oh yes,' said Mrs Roberts. 'I saw an advertisement in my magazine. It was for Paris breaks. They say you can travel there and back and stay in a really nice hotel for £149 per person, including continental breakfast, a complimentary map, a discount voucher for perfume and transport in an air conditioned coach between the railway station and the hotel on both arrival and on departure.'

It was generally agreed that this seemed a splendid idea, and very good value, and Mrs Roberts hurried to her room to find the magazine concerned.

She was back in moments, clutching the magazine which was already opened at the appropriate page.

'Ooh look, there's a picture of that tall tower thing they never finished building!' said Mrs Torridge peering over Mrs Roberts' shoulder.

Mrs Torridge had good days and bad days and was having one of her middling sort of days. 'All they've done is put up the scaffolding,' she added

'The French don't work hard like we do,' said Mr Roxdale firmly.

'They don't do any work after lunch,' explained Mr Livingstone. 'They all have a siesta in the afternoon.'

'I'm pretty sure that's the Eiffel Tower,' said Mrs Roberts, largely to Mrs Torridge but also just in case anyone else was wondering. 'It's all finished,' she added.

'So why don't they use a picture of it finished instead of a picture of it with the scaffolding up?' asked Mrs Torridge.

Mrs Roberts started to reply, realised that this was probably not going to get her very much further forward and so abandoned the thought.

'I think they have siestas in Spain,' said Mrs Torridge. 'I had one of them once when I was on holiday. They make them with red wine and lots of fruit. I suppose they're very nice if you like foreign drinks. I think they put lettuce in them. Definitely, they put in something green. The foreigners over there eat lots of rice and octopus too.'

'Oh we won't have to eat octopus will we?' asked Ruth. She shivered at the thought. She liked food but didn't like the idea of eating an octopus. She rather preferred a nice plate of chips and two fried eggs. How could you be sure the octopus wouldn't come alive, wrap a tentacle around your throat and eat you instead? She shivered at the thought. She had heard that the French ate frogs, snails and horses. But octopus? And what was the plural? Did you have two octopuses? Or two octopi?

'Isn't that drink with the fruit in it called sangria?' asked Mrs Merivale.

'Is it?' said Mrs Torridge, frowning. 'So if the drink is a sangria, what's a siesta?'

'Maybe that's the dish with the octopus and the rice,' said Miss Nightingale.

'Mint. I think it may have been mint not lettuce,' said Mrs Torridge thoughtfully. 'Or perhaps it was something else green. What's green?'

'Grass,' suggested Mr Roxdale.

'I've got some green socks,' said Mr Livingstone, helpfully. 'They're very comfortable but there's a hole in the heel of one of them. And I wouldn't put them into a drink.'

'We used to say we had a potato in our sock when we had a bit of heel showing,' said Mr Roxdale.

Mr Livingstone laughed. 'I remember that! At school we used to take off our socks to see who had the biggest potato.'

Mrs Torridge gave these suggestions due consideration. 'No,' she said at last. 'It wasn't grass or socks.'

'Why did Mr Roxdale say he had a potato in his sock?' asked Ruth, who couldn't quite understand how the potatoes had snuck into the conversation.

'When you have a bit of heel showing through a hole in a sock it looks a bit like a new potato,' explained Mrs Roberts.

Ruth, who didn't understand, nodded as though she did.

'Octopus and rice,' said Mrs Peterborough who liked the sound of this. She said it again.

It was no longer her regular custom to repeat what other people said but from time to time the habit reappeared. Since her drug regime had been reduced, she had also largely abandoned her endearing habit of mimicking what other people said and how they behaved.

Anyone who had known Mrs Peterborough, and the other residents of the Twilight Years Rest Home, back in the days when it had been run by the deeply unpleasant and unpopular Mr Hawksmoor, would have found it difficult to believe that this was the same woman.

Chapter Three

Under Mr Hawksmoor's authoritarian regime, the residents of what had then been known as The Twilight Years Rest Home had been kept heavily sedated in order to make them easier to look after. The law in Britain allows nursing and care home owners the right to medicate residents without their knowledge and even against their will, and Mr Hawksmoor had taken full advantage of this curious entitlement. The phrase 'it's for our own good' must be one of the most commonly uttered in all residential establishments catering for the elderly.

It is well known in medical circles that the symptoms of most of the dementias, including Dr Alzheimer's eponymous disorder (which is one of the commonest causes of dementia but by no means the only one) are exacerbated by an absence of mental and social stimulus. 'Old age puts more wrinkles in our minds than on our faces,' wrote Michel de Montaigne.

The precise pathological causes of dementia in general and Alzheimer's in particular, are still a subject of much discussion among doctors and research scientists. Despite much tub thumping, a good deal of it designed to attract the attention of people handing out grant money, researchers have not yet progressed beyond the stage of offering a seemingly infinite number of updates on a seemingly infinite number of hypotheses. But there does not seem to be much doubt that when sufferers are drugged, abandoned without stimulation or left to vegetate in dull and inspiring surroundings, their symptoms will deteriorate. The body and the mind, like any partners, do not always fail together and it can be argued that the mind is even more vulnerable than the body to a lack of exercise. We grow old more through inactivity and a lack of direction and purpose than through age itself.

The tragedy, of course, is that despite the fact that this knowledge is widely available, the staff in hospitals, nursing homes, rest homes, care homes and all the other residential centres, often act as though they are completely unaware of any of this. Maybe these establishments are so chronically understaffed that no one has the time to spare to ensure that brains are kept stimulated. Maybe no one cares. Maybe too many of those who are yet to tiptoe into the foothills of old age are still able to deny to themselves the inevitability that they too will one day grow old. One of the greatest contradictions in life is that although almost everyone wants to live a long time, no one wants to grow old. It is, perhaps, easier for some professionals to regard old age as another country and to dismiss old people as another species. And yet surely those who have taken on the responsibility for the elderly have a responsibility to ensure that they retain their faculties for as long as possible?

'Bodily decay is gloomy in prospect,' said Thomas Jefferson, the third President of the US, 'but of all human contemplations, the most abhorrent is body without mind.'

It has been said, by someone wise and proudly blessed with a way with words, that we are all as young as we feel and although on the surface this may sound like one of those superficial bon mots usually dismissed as cracker-barrel philosophy, there is more truth to it than may generally be realised. Mrs Caldicot's chums would, if anyone had asked, have confessed that they all felt themselves to be somewhere between 18 and 22 years of age. In reality, of course, it had been a good half a century since any of them had been in that age bracket, but that was now the way they felt and that, to a large extent, is all that matters. Mrs Caldicot who would, a couple of years earlier, have owned to an age somewhere in the mid-300s, now felt herself to be approximately 19 and a half and quite happy to stay just there, thank you very much for asking.

Now, after some months of companionship, friendship and a freedom from unnecessarily onerous and nit picking rules, Mrs Caldicot's band of chums had changed almost beyond recognition. Individuals who had once been residents of a typically oppressive care home had been transformed by residency in a friendly private home where laughter was an ever welcome guest. At Caldicot House, the atmosphere was lively and on occasion quite perky. A lack of medication and a modest increase in responsibility had, of course, also helped. They all still looked rather elderly, of course. But there was now a sparkle in their eyes and they behaved more like young people than some young people do.

The Meridews, Maurice and Maple, looked after the kitchen and produced meals which were nutritionally invigorating without being dull, stodgy or too full of bean curd. Their experience in preparing meals for film crews had well prepared them for the need to satisfy appetites which range from those needing occasional titivating (Mr Roxdale) to those which simply needed to be assuaged and, from time to time, indulged. The only standard rule was that cabbage was banned from the menu. This may have been a tough break for what is a perfectly innocent and vitamin packed leafy green brassica but it was something that Mrs Caldicot and the residents felt as one about. If you don't have any cabbage in a kitchen then the rooms which are supplied by that kitchen cannot possibly be flavoured with the ever present aroma of cabbage. Egg and chips and spotted dick with custard were no longer regarded as unsuitable fare, and crumpets and teacakes now played an important part in the daily diet both at tea-time and at supper time. Mr Livingstone had proved himself able to demolish a whole plateful of buttered crumpets all by himself.

The garden was looked after by Mr Hewitt and Mr Roxdale.

As already mentioned, Mr Twist took care of the accounts and, where necessary, income tax forms for everyone living in Caldicot House.

Mr Livingstone was in charge of musical entertainment and, in view of his experience as a valued member of RAF Bomber Command during the Second World War, had appointed himself in charge of defence and, in this regard, had taken on responsibility for ensuring that the front and back doors were locked at night.

Mrs Peterborough, Miss Nightingale and Mrs Torridge were in charge of the laundry and looked after the washing machine and the pegging out and bringing in of items placed upon the clothes line. (None of them had worked out how to operate the tumble dryer. This was, as they say, a 'good thing' since, as Mrs Torridge pointed out, it costs nothing to allow washing to dry on a clothes line but a good deal to force it to dry in an electrically heated machine.)

Mr Williams was the official photographer and always happy to sell one of his old photographs and give the proceeds to Mrs Caldicot when cash was running a little low. He was also responsible for keeping the house library well stocked with books and DVDs – some of which he purchased from local charity shops and some of which he ordered from local stores. He insisted on paying for all his purchases himself.

'But I don't know why they didn't use lettuce,' said Mrs Torridge. 'I've always liked a nice piece of lettuce though Mr Torridge, my late husband, couldn't stand the stuff bless his soul. He didn't like fruit in his drinks either. I remember that for a joke someone put two slices of orange in his beer and he was very cross.'

'So what do you all think about a trip to Paris?' asked Mrs Caldicot, who thought she ought to try to drag the conversation back from the surreal to the practical. Although she had always wanted to visit Paris, she felt that the decision should be made in a roughly democratic sort of way.

'How many stars does the hotel have?' asked Mrs Merivale, who, in the course of her work with the film industry, had stayed in a good many hotels and, as a result, put great store by the number of stars a hotel had been awarded.

Mrs Roberts picked up her magazine. 'The advertisement says: 'You will enjoy four star accommodation in a central location and you will be whisked from the Gare du Nord to your hotel in an air conditioned coach with a bilingual driver. And throughout your stay, our friendly and knowledgeable Representative will be on hand to ensure that everything on your holiday goes smoothly.'

'Crumbs,' said Mrs Merivale. 'You can't grumble at that, can you?' She turned to Mr Merivale. 'Did you hear that? Four stars.'

'Very acceptable,' confirmed Mr Merivale who had also travelled a good deal and once claimed he had stayed in as many hotels as he'd had hot dinners. 'You get a much better class of bedbug in four star hotels.'

'Wonderful,' said Mr Roxdale dryly. 'That'll be a comfort.'

And so it was agreed by the assembled company that they would all go to Paris together. They all agreed it would be wonderful to go on holiday in a group. Several of the group had seen a documentary about the French capital and all were excited by the prospect of seeing the Eiffel Tower, the Champs-Élysées and Sacre Coeur. It would, thought Mrs Caldicot, be a relaxing but also invigorating change for them all. She looked forward to being away from pressure and stress for a few days.

'Does anyone speak French?' asked Mr Twist.

'I learned French at school,' said Mr Livingstone, as though his school studies had enabled him to master the language and ignoring the fact that his school days had been considerably more than half a century previously. 'Bon voyage, mon brave,' he announced with confidence. 'La plume de ma tante est dans le bureau de…' At this point he hesitated, forgetting perhaps the nature of the ownership of the desk wherein resided the pen of his fortunate aunt.

'…mon oncle,' said Mr Williams, finishing the sentence for him. Everyone looked at Mr Williams. He shrugged. 'I know a few words,' he explained. 'I can get by,' he added modestly.

'I think I remember studying French at school,' said Mr Twist. 'It will probably all come flooding back once we get over there.' He paused, closed his eyes and dredged his memory. 'Le chat c'est assis sur le … mat,' he announced proudly. 'There you are! It's all in there just waiting to come bursting out. Je demande du fromage, du pain et du vin.'

'Do you remember Bertram Mills?' asked Mr Roxdale.

'I've heard of him,' said Mr Twist. 'He had a circus didn't he?'

'A very famous circus,' said Mr Roxdale. 'Mr Mills travelled the world, and I remember I once saw him being interviewed and the chap asking the questions asked Mr Mills if he had ever learned any foreign languages. He replied: 'When I get among foreigners I stand still, look British and shout!' So that is what I intend to do.'

With confidence born of ignorance and a newly found natural sense of communal optimism, it was generally agreed that with Mr Twist, Mr Livingstone and Mr Williams to look after the language problem, and to provide translating services for the rest of the party, there would be no difficulty in communicating successfully with the French natives.

Mrs Caldicot alone was slightly sceptical.

Nevertheless, she thought, it would be something of an adventure and there were bound to be one or two French people around who spoke English.

And anyway, she added to herself, a life without adventures is a dull life indeed.

Chapter Four

'So Mrs Roberts telephoned the advertisers and made a provisional booking for us all to go to Paris for three nights over the Easter holidays,' said Mrs Caldicot, who was now in the flat she shared with her husband and who was, therefore, technically Mrs Jenkins.

'Isn't that exciting?' she continued. 'Of course, we can't actually book the holiday until the cheque comes through from the lottery people. But Mrs Roberts spoke to a nice, young lady at the lottery who said we should have the cheque by the end of the week. We were surprised the holiday company had a vacancy over Easter but apparently another group had to cancel their trip because of an outbreak of something or other unfortunate and so we've inherited their train tickets and hotel bookings.'

'The lottery people don't have to send people around to bring you the cheque and warn you not to spend it all at once on champagne and Ferraris?' said Mr Jenkins.

'Oh no,' said Mrs Caldicot, earnestly. 'I think that's only for the big winners.'

'I was teasing,' said Mr Jenkins gently.

Mrs Caldicot threw a cushion at him. 'It's going to be like a second honeymoon!' she said. The cushion missed by a yard and a half. Mrs Caldicot's cat, Kitty, who was apparently asleep on the hearth rug, opened an eye, looked up and then went back to sleep.

Mr Jenkins looked at her questioningly.

'Yes, well there will be 12 other people with us and one or two of them probably needing a little looking after,' admitted Mrs Caldicot.

'You'll have your hands full,' promised Mr Jenkins.

'I'll have Mrs Roberts and Ruth to help me,' said Mrs Caldicot.

Mr Jenkins smiled but didn't say anything. Secretly he rather wondered if an SAS regiment would provide enough manpower and experience to keep Mrs Caldicot's companions out of trouble. Still, he had faith in his wife. She had long ago proved herself capable, competent and sensitive to the needs of the former nursing home residents who had become her very dear friends.

Mrs Caldicot, who had been contemplating the trip through slightly less rosy spectacles, sighed quietly. 'You're right,' she said. 'I'm probably going to be rather busy. You don't think it's a silly idea, do you?'

'Not at all!' insisted Mr Jenkins who knew Paris well, having visited it frequently when working as a newspaper editor. 'It will be an adventure. You'll be spending part of the week before Easter in Paris: wonderful food, bright lights and probably some sunshine. The weather is usually good in Paris in April.' He chuckled as he thought of something. 'We must have a dozen oysters each while we're there,' he said. 'There's a famous restaurant opposite the Gare du Nord that serves the best oysters in France.'

'Oysters?' said Mrs Caldicot, who wasn't a great fan of slithery food.

'Well, we'll be there at Easter. So we'll have to celebrate with our own Oyster Parade won't we?'

Mrs Caldicot, who was still not entirely accustomed to her husband's puns, winced.

'I'm pleased that we're going by train and not by aeroplane,' said Mr Jenkins. 'People get on an aeroplane and a few hours later they are in another country – on another continent even. Going abroad used to be a Great Adventure. There was the train to Dover, a long walk to the boat across the Channel to Calais and then another walk through the customs shed to the French train which would be sitting waiting to whisk travellers to Paris. Mark Twain, Charles Dickens, Arnold Bennett – they all did it and they all wrote about the sense of excitement that built as the journey progressed. Travellers had a chance to realise that they were going somewhere new; time to prepare themselves for the adventures ahead; time to enjoy the differences between there and here. Of course, Dover and Calais were grubby, grey, shabby and unprepossessing but in a way all that squalor and shabbiness added to the experience. You knew that you were seeing things that countless thousands of travellers had seen for generations. You felt like a traveller rather than a tourist.'

'Unfortunately, we don't go on a boat,' Mrs Caldicot reminded her husband. 'The train goes through a tunnel underneath the Channel.'

'Yes, there is that,' said Jenkins, with more than a little sadness 'I shall miss the docks at Dover and at Calais. But it's still a train. It's considerably more exciting than an aeroplane journey. I loathe aeroplanes and airports.' He shuddered. He had spent much of the previous three decades travelling through airports and sitting on aeroplanes. 'Have you fixed a date?' he asked.

Mrs Caldicot told him and added. 'Those were the only dates they had available for a party of 14. And we got a special, special rate because we took over a last minute cancellation.'

Mr Jenkins, who was rather old-fashioned and liked to keep his appointments listed somewhere out of the range of hackers, software failures and battery outages, took a slim, leather pocket diary from his inside pocket and consulted it. The procedure, Jenkins liked to point out, took rather less time than it would have taken a more technologically minded individual to turn on their computer or to scroll through their mobile telephone. And he liked the feel of the leather and the crackle of the paper.

'Ah,' he said, rather sadly. 'I'm afraid there will only be 13 of you. But if you only have a provisional booking you'll be able to cancel my ticket and take the proceeds as spending money for the trip.'

'You can't come?' said Mrs Caldicot, horrified.

'I'm afraid not,' said Mr Jenkins, who was genuinely upset to be missing the trip. For one thing he wanted to be able to help his wife if, or when, one of the residents got into trouble. And for another he loved his wife very much indeed and didn't like to be away from her for more than an hour or two at a time.

'I agreed to chair a discussion group at a literary festival that week,' he explained. 'I did tell you about it some time ago. I've agreed to do it and I'm afraid I really can't back out now. I'll only be away for one day but it's right in the middle of your trip.' He paused for a moment, a thought having occurred to him. 'Actually, it's probably just as well. If we were all away who would look after Kitty?'

Although he was retired, Mr Jenkins, a former newspaper editor, was much in demand. He was a fluent and personable speaker and had written a couple of books about modern journalism. He was frequently invited to speak at literary festivals, now something of a boom industry in the peripheries of the publishing world, and he was a regular broadcaster on the wireless, as he insisted on calling it, and on the moving picture show of television.

'Oh that's awful!' said Mrs Caldicot, who was as disappointed as she sounded. 'I'll ask Mrs Roberts to see if she can change the dates.'

'You'll do no such thing,' insisted Mr Jenkins. 'You know she only got that booking because of a cancellation. It will probably be months before you can get another suitable date. And everyone will be disappointed if they have to wait months for their holiday. Besides, I tell you what we'll do. We'll use the fee I'm being paid by the literary festival for a slap-up romantic dinner for just the two of us when you get back. No expense spared.'

'I suppose you're right,' said Mrs Caldicot, looking for a silver lining to the cloud. 'It does mean that you will be able to look after Kitty.'

'Kitty and I will look after each other. I'll give her dishes of milk and plates of food and she'll keep my lap warm while I work on page one of my novel. Doubtless she will purr me to sleep before I get onto the unknown territory of page two.'

'You're just as big a softy as I am!' said Mrs Caldicot. It suddenly occurred to her that without her husband accompanying the party she'd be able to forgo the oysters. It was a small consolation, but a consolation, nevertheless.

'Don't you dare tell anyone,' warned Mr Jenkins very sternly.

And so, four days later, the booking was confirmed, the holiday company was paid and the trip to Paris was upgraded from a pencilled in, provisional booking to a fully confirmed etched in stone arrangement. Mr Jenkins's ticket had been cancelled and the proceeds added by Mrs Caldicot to their spending money. They would leave England on a Tuesday, stay in Paris on Tuesday, Wednesday and Thursday nights, and return home on the Friday.

Chapter Five

As the time of their trip to Paris approached, so the excitement mounted.

Mrs Torridge, Mrs Peterborough and Miss Nightingale spent many happy hours deciding which of their clothes they would take. In the end they all decided that, to be on the safe side, they would be better off taking everything. They therefore scoured the building and collected a mass of old suitcases, bags and containers into which they could cram their belongings.

Ruth, booked a visit to the beauty salon to spend everything in her current account, and a little bit more, on having her hair cut and tinted, her nails professionally painted and her legs waxed almost but not quite up to her bikini line. (She decided against what is in the trade known as a Brazilian Wax only after Mrs Roberts had assured her that Paris is not by the sea and that they would definitely not be spending their days in France sunbathing or visiting swimming pools.)

Mr Hewitt announced that he would be taking his trowel, hand fork and hand-carved wooden dibber since it was his experience that you never knew when these items would come in handy and the last thing you wanted was to find yourself short of a dibber when you really needed one.

Mr Livingstone and Mr Twist spent their days polishing their schoolboy French and the Merivales bought, checked and packed a portable coffee making machine, a travel iron and a new suitcase on wheels.

Mrs Caldicot, alerted to the decision made by Mrs Torridge, Mrs Peterborough and Miss Nightingale issued a stern warning that every member of the party would be limited to one suitcase and one small piece of hand luggage.

She knew, however, that it is not the difficulties you foresee that cause the headaches. The things you worry about most usually turn out to be of little consequence. It is the problems you don't see coming which really hit you hard on the back of the neck.

Mrs Caldicot's ruling meant that it was back to the drawing board for Mrs Torridge, Mrs Peterborough and Miss Nightingale.

It was Mrs Torridge's idea that they should send Ruth into town to purchase for them the three largest suitcases she could find. Since it was impossible for her to carry all three suitcases onto a bus, Ruth had to travel back home in a taxi which cost Mrs Caldicot £9.50 or £10.00 with the tip.

Even when completely empty the suitcases she brought back were too heavy for any of the residents to lift.

Chapter Six

It has for many years been customary for travelling sports teams to take with them a baggage master – an individual whose task it is to ensure that the party's luggage travels with them and does not get diverted, stolen, mislaid, distracted or left behind. When there is a baggage master attached to a party, all the other members of the group can relax. They do not have to worry about losing a bag en route.

Naturally, Mrs Caldicot and her entourage did not have a baggage master.

And as she supervised the loading of the luggage into the small coach which had been hired to take them to the railway station, from whence they would board a train which would take them all on to London, St Pancras and the Eurostar train to Paris, Mrs Caldicot could not help but think that life would have been considerably easier if she had been supervising the travels of the England Football team on a trip to the other side of the globe. At least she would have then had the assistance of a specialist baggage master. And, as a footnote to this thought, she wondered idly if the England Football team took as much luggage with them when they travelled as her own little group.

The main problem was that despite her entreaties, the members of her party had packed as if they were going away for three months, rather than for five days and three nights.

Mrs Caldicot tried to console herself, and to gain some small comfort, from the knowledge that Aristocratic Victorian travellers, rich on the backs of mill workers, miners and other indentured skivvies, used to go on their Continental tours equipped with several hundred pieces of luggage containing every convenience, necessity and luxury known to man, woman or child.

No Duke, Earl or even a paltry Baronet would dare set foot further south than Dover without a full range of warming pans, butterfly nets, pith helmets, climbing boots, tin baths and other essentials.

But then she remembered that those same Victorian travellers invariably took with them a small army of servants and that it was by no means unknown for a travelling peer off on a mind-broadening Grand Tour, or an artefact collecting expedition, to be accompanied by more than 100 maids, footmen, butlers, cooks and strong men to carry the bags.

The thought with which she had tried to comfort herself faded into nothing more than useless, outdated trivia.

Mrs Caldicot herself had packed the cases for Mrs Torridge, Mrs Peterborough and Miss Nightingale and, not knowing what sort of weather to expect, she had included a choice of clothing for warm, wet or cold weather.

But having decided that Mrs Caldicot had been far too cautious, indeed conservative, the trio had insisted on opening their suitcases and cramming in just about everything else they could find which seemed remotely suitable for a trip to Paris.

Mrs Torridge's mammoth sized suitcase now contained seven pairs of shoes, two pairs of slippers, a large hat and a large teddy bear who had a red ribbon round his neck and just one remaining eye and was, for reasons long ago lost in the mists of time, known as Cuthbert.

Mrs Peterborough had packed six skirts, five dresses, an evening gown with sequins and two hats, one with feathers and one without. She had managed to cram in a dressing gown, seven nightdresses and a pair of pyjamas. She had also popped in a yellow plastic bucket and a small spade which she'd found at the back of the garage and which had been leftover from a day trip to the seaside. 'But we're going on holiday!' she protested, when Mrs Roberts pointed out that Paris is not on the coast. 'I always used to take a bucket and spade with me when I went away on holiday.'

Miss Nightingale, more concerned with the inner woman than outward appearances, and having once heard that French dietary preferences tend to hover around the sort of things that are normally found slithering or hopping around the garden, had crammed her suitcase full to the brim with many tins of food (mainly mulligatawny soup, apricots in syrup and pilchards) numerous packets of biscuits and a dozen bars of chocolate. She had also popped in three long playing records. She was not intending to play these, not having packed a record player, but she had slid them into the case simply because she had found that she was able to fit them in. 'Mustn't waste space,' she had said to Mrs Peterborough. Despite the inclusion of all this food, she had managed to cram in a number of winter woollies, her entire collection of woolly hats and a variety of other clothing items.

Sadly, although Miss Nightingale did not know this, the biscuits had not survived. They had been in the suitcase when Mrs Peterborough had sat on it so that Miss Nightingale could close it properly. And Mrs Peterborough's bottom versus the biscuits had proved to be an unequal battle.

Where once there had been biscuits now there were crumbs.

The male members of the party were no better at restraining themselves from excess.

Mr Roxdale had packed his favourite twelve volume set of gardening encyclopaedias ('something to read on the train'), his Wellington boots ('don't want to get mud on my best shoes and it often rains a good deal in these foreign places') and a variety of gardening implements ('the French don't understand gardening because it involves hard work and so there will probably be a park that needs my attention').

Mr Hewitt, also a keen gardener, had, as had previously disclosed, packed his favourite trowel, hand fork and dibber but he had also crammed three economy sized boxes of cornflakes, a loaf of sliced bread, two family sized packs of bacon and two boxes each containing 12 eggs into his suitcase.

Mr Hewitt rather liked an English breakfast and wasn't going to start the day on nothing more substantial than a flaky croissant. He was also determined that no one else was going to have to go without a proper breakfast.

Mr Livingstone, in contrast, had a modestly sized suitcase but he also had three instrument cases for he insisted on travelling with his flute, his banjo and a set of African bongo drums.

Only Mrs Caldicot, Mrs Roberts and Ruth had restrained themselves and taken the more usual variety of essential stuff for the holiday. But, as Mrs Caldicot confessed to her husband, there was an inevitable sense of self-preservation in this since all three of them were well aware that they would probably be doing the lion's share of carrying suitcases and bags.

The result was that loading all the luggage into the hold of the coach which had been booked to take them to the railway station took rather longer than Mrs Caldicot had expected and required a considerable amount of rearranging and huffing and cursing by the driver.

'You didn't tell me you were moving house,' the driver complained with what he, but no one else, thought of as searing wit.

Mr Jenkins, who was there to help and to say goodbye to Mrs Caldicot (they both hated the idea of railway station partings) solved the problem by handing the driver a crisp, new £20 note, telling him that in return for this small 'pourboire', he expected help in unloading the luggage when the coach arrived at the railway station where, of course, the whole procedure had to be conducted in reverse.

That early part of the journey all went remarkably smoothly.

The coach took them to the local railway station.

A local stopping train took them up to London.

And in London a coach which had been booked to take them all to St Pancras was, to Mrs Caldicot's ill-concealed surprise, exactly where it was supposed to be.

And then the party had to find and clamber aboard the Eurostar train to St Pancras.

Naturally, there were no porters or trolleys to be seen and Mrs Caldicot, Mrs Roberts and Ruth and the others had to carry their impedimenta further than they would have chosen. Naturally, the escalator was not working and so the bags and cases had to be hauled up a seemingly interminable staircase. And then everything had to be dragged and pulled along a platform to the coach where their seats were booked. Mr Livingstone reckoned they had carried their bags for at least a mile and a half.

Finally, they had to load most of the luggage onto the train themselves. Three clipboard carrying employees stood and watched.

'Why aren't there any trolleys?' asked Mrs Roberts, pausing for a moment as she struggled to heave another suitcase up the high steps and into the carriage.

'Health and safety,' explained one of the clipboard owners. 'A woman was banged on the ankle by a trolley so we have to keep them all locked up.'

'We should have done some training,' muttered a breathless Mrs Roberts. 'Dragging the luggage up and down the stairs a few times perhaps.'

'Dragging everything down into town and then back again would have been a good test,' said a red-faced Ruth.

'Against the clock,' said Mrs Roberts.

'I should have insisted that everyone throw out at least half of the stuff in their cases,' said Mrs Caldicot wearily.

'And then thrown out half of what was left,' said Mrs Roberts.

By the time they slumped into their reserved seats, they were all exhausted.

'This luggage is going to prove to be something of a problem,' said Mrs Caldicot to Mrs Roberts and Ruth.

They both agreed that she was almost certainly correct.

'I really should have had a firm word with Mr Livingstone about those instrument cases,' said Mrs Caldicot. 'I did say only one suitcase and one piece of hand-luggage.'

'What on earth is he taking those for?' asked Mrs Roberts.

'I've no idea,' said Mrs Caldicot.

'Miss Nightingale's suitcase feels as though she's filled it with lead,' said Ruth, who rather thought she might have strained something vital in heaving the case onto the train. She was trying to work out how many more times she would have to help move all the luggage. There would be once when they got off the train at the Gare du Nord. And then, unless they could find a porter or a trolley of some kind, the cases would have to be dragged across the station concourse. Then the luggage would have to be loaded onto the travel company's coach. And it would have to be taken off the coach when it arrived at their hotel.

Her muscles ached at the thought of it all.

Still, maybe a gallant Frenchman would take pity on her, help with the luggage and then whisk her off for a five course dinner at an absurdly glamorous and expensive restaurant. She closed her eyes and dreamt of the candlelit restaurant, the attentive waiters and the handsome, charming, slightly naughty Frenchman on the other side of the flower arrangement on their cosy table for two. She must not, she thought, allow herself to drink too much champagne.

Ruth did a good deal of day-dreaming though she would have screamed for help and run a mile if any Frenchman (slightly naughty or not) had even suggested whisking her off to a glamorous and expensive restaurant.

'Oh dear,' said Mrs Caldicot, still worrying about Miss Nightingale's case. 'I hope she hasn't put in anything which will get her into trouble with the customs people.'

'Crumbs,' said Mrs Roberts. 'I'd forgotten all about customs. I hope they don't open any of our suitcases.'

'We can but hope,' said Mrs Caldicot who had learned not to lean too heavily on hope as a support.

'I think I'm about to have a rather late mid-life crisis,' said Mrs Roberts.

'I feel as though I've been having one of those since I was about 18,' said Mrs Caldicot. 'And I'm not finished with it yet.'

Chapter Seven

Sadly, the problems began before the cases were opened.

'All luggage to be putted onto the conveying belt,' ordered the man in a Border Control uniform, giving his best impression of a jackbooted Obergruppenfuhrer.

Mrs Caldicot rightly suspected that he wasn't paid very much but that he liked his job because he got a free uniform and every day he could be rude to people who didn't dare say anything back to him.

He clearly liked ordering people about.

The man looked like a bad tempered version of one of the larger animals found in zoos; the ones who live in enclosures festooned with signs saying 'Do Not Feed' and 'No Buns Allowed'. He was extremely foreign and in addition to not speaking very good English, he spoke with a curiously and unexpectedly strong Essex accent. Mrs Caldicot didn't like to say anything, of course, but she did secretly think it rather odd that England's borders should be protected by foreigners.

Looking around, she noticed that all the border control employees seemed to have soured expressions as though they never laughed and could not remember ever having seen anything to laugh at.

She wondered if they were selected for their facial expressions ('Customs Official wanted: must have sour look') or if they were hired, blank as it were, and then sent to a special training school where they were taught how to look stern, unforgiving and untrusting. Maybe, she thought, they are all former Post Office employees.

'And you are to be putting all metal objections inside the tray with which you be provided before going into the metal detector,' the man added, with a scowl.

Or he said something like that, anyway.

His accent was so strange that Mrs Caldicot had no real idea what he was saying. He could, she thought, have been reciting a recipe for cauliflower cheese.

'Say please!' said Miss Nightingale firmly. 'You must always say 'please'.'

'You should say 'please',' said Mrs Peterborough, who was next in the queue.

'Oh dear,' thought Mrs Caldicot.

It occurred to her that slightly dotty old ladies who appear perfectly normal from the outside can be a good more trouble than small children with behavioural disorders.

The customs man, clearly shocked that anyone should dare talk to him that way, if at all, stared at Mrs Peterborough as if she'd told him to take down his trousers or as though she had pulled a field howitzer out of her handbag.

He felt dismayed because if he were no longer allowed to be rude to travellers, there would be no joy at all in his life. In the movies he liked to watch in his spare time, the man in authority, and wearing a nice uniform, would only have to look sternly at the crowd, and maybe raise an admonitory hand, for the masses to fall silent in an instant.

That was how he saw himself: as the man in authority with an admonitory hand.

Moreover, these were old people.

He saw wrinkled, weak, frail bodies and assumed, for no reason other than old-fashioned prejudice, that the minds inside those bodies must also be weak and frail.

Miss Nightingale had shattered all his illusions and left him reeling.

Two yards away, Mrs Torridge was slowly edging her walking frame towards the metal detector gate. It was a slow business. Unless she was sitting on the mobility scooter, Mrs Torridge didn't go anywhere in a hurry. A small queue had formed behind her. Mrs Torridge couldn't really understand why they had a door frame without a door in it but everything around her was too noisy and too frantic for her to worry too much about this.

And so she edged forwards, inch by inch.

'It's only polite to say 'please',' insisted Miss Nightingale to the man at the customs post. 'What did your mother tell you to say?'

'What did your mother tell you to say?' demanded Mrs Peterborough. She folded her arms across her chest and glared at the man. Mrs Peterborough was normally a jolly woman but she could, when it seemed necessary, look down her nose and over her spectacles as well as anyone.

'In England we are taught to be polite to one another,' said Miss Nightingale who had decided that they must have already arrived in France. She spoke loudly and slowly so as to make it easier for to the man to understand since it had not entirely escaped her ken that, doubtless as a result of having rather substandard educational systems, not all foreigners spoke fluent English.

The customs officer, who had gone an unpleasant and unhealthy looking shade of puce, pulled himself up to his full five foot two and a little bit inches (including built-up shoes) and glared at them both. No one other than his superior, his wife, his mother and his three children had ever spoken to him in such a fearless manner.

Meanwhile, there was a good deal of noise coming from another part of the customs area.

'You can't go through with that!' shouted another foreigner in a Border Control uniform. He was very fat, frowned constantly and had a shifty, constantly guilty, look about him. Mrs Caldicot suspected that even his mother would probably admit he looked like the guilty one in a police line-up of sex offenders. There are always some men who join the army because they want to kill people without getting into trouble. And there are customs officers who put on their uniform each day looking forward to bringing a little darkness into ordinary people's lives. This customs officer looked like the sort of man who had taken the job because he didn't like people very much.

He had spotted that Mrs Torridge and her walking frame were about to pass through the metal detector.

'Why not?' demanded Mrs Torridge, confused and indignant in equal proportions. 'It's the only way I can get to my bag!' She took one hand off her walking frame and pointed to her luggage which was waiting for her at the end of the conveyor belt. Holding onto her walking frame with one hand was for her the equivalent of riding a bicycle one handed.

'We have to examine your stick thing!' insisted the fat Border Control officer.

And with that he snatched the walking frame from Mrs Torridge.

Mrs Caldicot stared in disbelief.

It occurred to her that maybe the prize pupils from Post Office training establishments were picked out for Border control work. ('You are one of our prize pupils Miss Taj Mahal. You are the rudest person we've seen for years. The Border Control people would like you to work for them.')

Since Mrs Torridge was leaning heavily on the walking frame at the time, the result of this confiscation was inevitable.

Mrs Torridge stood still for a moment and then, very slowly, started to rock backwards and forwards. Mrs Caldicot, who was trying to keep an eye on everyone, watched in horror. Everything seemed to happen in slow motion. It was clear that Mrs Torridge was about to fall but the only question was: would she fall backwards or would she fall forwards.

In the end she fell backwards; collapsing with surprising grace; and subsiding to a heap on the floor in a slow motion movement that a ballet dancer would have envied.

'Put your metal objects into the tray!' shouted the first foreigner, who had not noticed Mrs Torridge's subsidence and probably wouldn't have cared much if he had. 'I am workings for the Border Force and so I do not have to be saying of 'please' to you!'

'Don't be so rude!' shouted Mrs Peterborough who, misled by the man's strange accent, had now also decided that they must have arrived in France and that she was, therefore, addressing a person of French origin. She knew that when speaking to foreigners one should always speak loudly, slowly and clearly so that they can understand.

She also admonished the man by gently smacking him on the arm as a mother might tap a child.

Startled, the man backed away and shouted for help.

A few yards away Mrs Torridge, who was lying flat on her back on the floor, was also shouting. She was calling: 'Will someone please help me up?' The fat Border Control officer who was examining Mrs Torridge's walking frame ignored her because helping old ladies up off the floor wasn't part of his job description.

Mrs Caldicot, abandoned Miss Nightingale and Mrs Peterborough and, having collected Ruth, who had been about to help put Mr Livingstone's array of musical instruments onto the conveyor belt, set off to help Mrs Torridge who was still lying on the floor, floundering and doing a pretty good impersonation of a fish out of water. The travellers who had been queuing behind her pretended that she wasn't there and stepped around her, and in one case over her, in order to pass through the metal detecting archway.

As she rushed forward to help Mrs Torridge, Mrs Caldicot was elbowed aside by two heavily armed policemen who were responding to the cry from the customs officer who had suffered a slight smack on the arm from a slightly dotty septuagenarian and who was already thinking of the compensation and damages he could claim from his employers after Mrs Peterborough had been arrested, charged, tried, found guilty and imprisoned.

The two policemen, neither of whom looked to be more than 15-years-old, though Mrs Caldicot thought they could, perhaps, have been young looking 16-year-olds, were both brandishing automatic weapons. One of the policemen was male and the other was not. Both were growing moustaches but the female police person was having considerably more success with hers which had already acquired a luxuriousness which her partner's upper lip seemed unlikely to be able to match.

'Down on the floor!' yelled the boy policemen. He was trying hard not to panic but not doing very well at it. He had acne and a lisp and was very conscious of his moustache which he fingered at least once a minute to check that it was still growing nicely. 'Everyone get down on the floor with your hands behind your backs.'

Some people can command battalions with a single barked order. Unfortunately, this policeman had one of those strange squeaky voices which never command much in the way of respect.

Still, when you are one of the few people in a room to have an automatic weapon a certain amount of respect is inevitably forthcoming. A young mother started to scream. Her six children, loyal to the echo, all followed suit.

'Mrs Torridge has been mugged!' cried Mr Livingstone, who hadn't seen anything of what had happened but who now saw Mrs Torridge lying on the floor. He and Mr Roxdale tried to step around behind the second policemen in order to help their friend to her feet. The second policeman was so tall that she didn't ever really know where her feet were, or what they were up to, until a few minutes after they'd finished moving. This made tennis, dancing and other similar activities frustrating, disappointing and something of a hazard. It also gave her an instability that sometimes interfered with her ability to stand firm and tall in the pursuit of justice. Sensing movement behind her, the tall policeman stepped to one side and immediately fell over Mrs Torridge. She landed with quite a thump and lay winded on her chest with her automatic gun underneath her.

The male policeman, the one who had the strange, squeaky voice, was proud of his peripheral vision, and he immediately noticed that his partner was now on the floor where the terrorists should normally be. He swung round to help. As he did so he collided with Mr Livingstone, tripped over Mr Livingstone's banjo case and crashed into the conveyor belt used to carry luggage (and musical instruments) through the X-ray machine. His automatic weapon ended up on the conveyor belt and he ended up on the floor.

'Are you all right, Mrs Torridge?' asked Mrs Caldicot, who had finally fought her way to her friend.

'I think so,' replied Mrs Torridge. 'But my dignity has definitely been injured. Am I decent?' she tried to look down to check that her dress was still properly aligned.

Mrs Caldicot assured her that nothing untoward was on display.

'This is why my mother always told me to make sure I was wearing clean ones,' whispered Mrs Torridge.

Mrs Caldicot smiled at her and with Ruth's help, helped her to her feet. Mrs Torridge clung to the frame surrounding the door that wasn't there and rubbed her thigh where she had landed on the floor.

Mr Twist was always nervous of policemen, even when they were growing moustaches and one of them had a strange, squeaky voice. Not even the fact that both policemen were now lying on the floor lessened his anxiety. He therefore lay down on the floor, face up so that he could see what was going on, and then tried to put his hands behind his back. He found that lying this way was very uncomfortable but it was, he thought, what the policeman had told him to do and so he did it. The ever reliable Mrs Roberts, as calm and phlegmatic as ever, knelt down beside him and assured him that there was really nothing to worry about and that everything was going to be all right.

One or two other travellers, none of them in Mrs Caldicot's party, followed Mr Twist's example, and the floor of the customs area was soon full of people wriggling about trying to get comfortable. Half a dozen children were crying and, much to the distress of a man in a uniform who kept shouting that taking photographs was not allowed, a group of Japanese tourists who had absolutely no idea what was going on and assumed that the chaos was perfectly normal were lying on the floor giggling and taking photographs of one another.

'Officer down!' yelled the squeaky voiced policeman into his radio. He looked around for his gun which had now travelled into the bowels of the X-ray machine and had, therefore, apparently disappeared.

Strictly speaking, both officers were down and if he had thought about it more, a more accurate call for help would have been: 'Officers down'.

Of course, the word 'down' in police terms is normally utilised to describe an incident in which one or more policemen have been attacked and wounded rather than an incident in which two clumsy and slightly inept policemen have both tripped over and fallen all by themselves, but police procedure does not allow for such niceties and as far as the emergency room dispatcher was concerned, an officer was down and help was needed.

Meanwhile, the Border Control officer who was manning the X-ray machine suddenly noticed that something that looked suspiciously like an automatic weapon was sitting on his conveyor belt. He pressed his alarm button and started to yell for help.

Consequently, moments later every policeman in the building could be seen running towards the customs area. Laden as they were with their helmets, bullet proof vests, protective chest guards, thigh guards, elbow guards, guns, spare ammunition and lots of shiny accoutrements they looked red-faced and rather flushed by the time they arrived. Several of them, the ones who were particularly red-faced and perspiring, looked as though they had not been well-designed for urgent physical activity.

'What's going on?' demanded Mr Livingstone of no one in particular.

'Some sort of game, I think,' replied Mr Twist. He looked around and could see a small, nervous looking policeman trying to disentangle himself from Mr Livingstone's banjo case; a tall policewoman trying to disentangle herself from the strap of her automatic weapon; a customs man examining Mrs Torridge's walking frame; a Border Control officer, who was sitting behind the X-ray machine, doing a very good impersonation of a man in a panic; a number of travellers lying on the floor, all with their hands in clear sight; Mrs Torridge clinging to a doorway which had no door; a Border Control official holding his arm as though it had been broken and a number of Border Control officials who looked as though they were having nervous breakdowns.

'Exercise,' said Mr Merivale firmly, as though he knew what he was talking about. 'It's definitely one of those training exercises. Like when they ring the alarm bell in a hotel and see how long it takes for everyone to get downstairs and gather together on the pavement in their nightwear.' Mr Merivale had taken one look at the floor, which he thought rather dirty, and was still standing.

The others nodded in agreement. An exercise was the only thing that made sense.

'They always do it in the middle of the night because it gives the staff a laugh,' said Mr Merivale, who knew about hotels. 'They like to see their guests in their night clothes, all shivering in the cold.'

'Do you think we'll ever get to Paris?' murmured Mrs Roberts, looking around at the chaos around them.

'It's not looking good,' replied Mrs Caldicot. She sighed. Not for the first time on their journey she wished Mr Jenkins was with them. She felt sure that he would know how to deal with things. It occurred to her that it was a good thing that they had arrived at St Pancras with plenty of time to spare. When she had made the initial arrangements, and looked at the various train times, she had imagined herself having time to sit with a leisurely cup of coffee and, perhaps, a Danish pastry, before boarding the Eurostar train. So far, it hadn't quite worked out that way.

It now looked as though she and her charges would need every minute of the extra time she had allowed in order to battle their way through the various customs procedures.

Chapter Eight

Sorting out the confusion and chaos in the customs area took just over an hour.

To begin with there was talk of arresting both Mrs Torridge (for attempting to take an unauthorised walking frame into the departure area at St Pancras) and Mrs Peterborough (for assaulting a Border Control officer) but a rare police inspector with his head screwed on the right way round decided that none of this would be in anyone's best interests. Not even he, however, had been able to prevent an over-enthusiastic officer from ringing the Bomb Squad and demanding that someone come and check out Mrs Torridge's aluminium walking frame.

The customs officer who had been so severely assaulted by Mrs Peterborough had gone off into a private room to share the details of his traumatic experience and to discuss his compensation claim with his union representative, a lawyer, a human resources expert, a public relations official and a psychiatrist drafted in to provide emergency counselling. There was already talk of an early retirement, a full disability pension and a lump sum payment in compensation. The only question seemed to be the size of the compensation payment and the wording of the press statement.

The two police officers who had ended up on the floor had gone off duty so that they could rest after their exhausting ordeal. When the police inspector eventually viewed video coverage of the entire incident, the two young officers were told to take a month's sick leave before attending an extensive debriefing with a review board. It was suggested to them that when they returned to work they might prefer to take up roles in traffic management. Overseeing a pedestrian crossing outside the station had been offered as a suitable site for their employment though it had been pointed out that they would need extensive and lengthy retraining before taking on this level of responsibility.

The small army of police officers who had responded so promptly to the 'Officer down' emergency call remained distributed throughout the area. They were still holding their automatic weapons at the ready but although they were not sure why they had been summoned, they were still alert and rather on the jumpy side of edgy. Mrs Caldicot's party of older travellers did not match the profile of modern-day terrorists but, as one officer pointed out, some terrorists can be masters of disguise and you can never be too careful. Several kept their guns aimed at Mrs Torridge who was deemed by an alert sergeant to be the possible ringleader of a gang of domestic insurgents.

Mrs Torridge's walking frame had been taken apart, examined and left in pieces by an explosives expert who had been given a police escort and had raced to St Pancras in a Bomb Squad Land Rover. It took Mr Livingstone and Mr Roxdale some time to put the walking frame back together and although it was still a little wobbly, it was more or less serviceable. Mrs Caldicot watched them with a smile and considerable pride. It was a joy to her to know that her companions were always loyal and willing to help one another.

The next step in the process of getting through customs involved the party's luggage.

This had been the part of the procedure which Mrs Caldicot had feared most.

'Open your suitcase,' said the customs officer to Miss Nightingale. The officer was a woman of indeterminate years who looked as if she had suffered from really bad irritable bowel syndrome for at least a decade and was currently struggling to cope with an intestinal storm or, possibly, a gastric hurricane. Mrs Caldicot thought she looked like a shop owner who on a wet January morning finds herself faced with a queue of people returning unwanted Christmas presents. She certainly did not look the sort of woman whose life was punctuated with gales of unbridled laughter. She had a wispy string of hair hanging down in front of her face and the result rather reminded Mrs Caldicot of the back end of a horse she had once put money on when she had spent a day at Newbury Races. The horse, Mrs Caldicot remembered, had finished its race a rather poor last; the jockey spattered with mud from having spent the entire time struggling to catch up with the rest of the field. She could not help thinking, but definitely did not say, that if Helen of Troy had a face that had launched 1,000 ships then this woman had a face that had probably launched 1,000 refuse carts.

'Say please,' said Miss Nightingale.

'It would help if you would say 'please',' murmured Mrs Caldicot to the customs officer. She didn't think her intervention would do much good but she thought she would try.

Heart sinking she had darted across to be by Miss Nightingale's side when she had seen that Miss Nightingale's case had been selected for investigation. The officer watching the case go through the X-ray machine, had been unable to make head nor tail of the contents which bore absolutely no resemblance to the sort of thing usually seen when holiday makers' suitcases were viewed on an X-ray machine.

'Stand away,' ordered the customs officer sternly. 'Who are you?'

'I'm a friend,' replied Mrs Caldicot. 'I'm a friend of Miss Nightingale's.'

'And who is Miss Nightingale when she is at home?' demanded the customs officer who was not afraid to share a cliché when one tottered into view.

'She's my friend,' explained Mrs Caldicot. 'It's her suitcase.'

'Open your suitcase, please,' mumbled the customs officer reluctantly. The use of the word 'please' clearly offended her professional susceptibilities but she had seen enough to realise that this group of travellers were potential trouble.

Miss Nightingale opened her suitcase.

The moment she did so the contents which had been compressed by having been sat on by Mrs Peterborough, sprang upwards in clear relief at having been freed from their confinement. Some spilt outwards onto the counter top and only swift action by Mrs Caldicot prevented a pair of pink Disneyland pyjamas sliding onto the floor. The pyjamas, which were Miss Nightingale's favourites, were decorated with pictures of Mickey and Minnie Mouse.

The customs officer began to unpack the suitcase.

Miss Nightingale, watching, looked at Mrs Caldicot.

'It's all right,' said Mrs Caldicot reassuringly. She smiled at Miss Nightingale. Mrs Caldicot was conscious of the fact that Miss Nightingale never liked having her belongings handled by strangers. Once, when a plumber had moved her dressing gown without asking her permission, she had attacked him with a pink, fluffy mule. The plumber, a 22-year-old Pole, had fled the scene and never returned.

'What's this?' demanded the customs officer, holding up a tin of Mulligatawny soup.

'That looks like soup,' said Mrs Caldicot, examining the label. 'My best guess, based on the information provided by the label, would be Mulligatawny.'

'Soup,' agreed Miss Nightingale, with a nod of her head.

'Please allow the owner of the suitcase to answer for herself,' said the customs officer pompously. She had come top in pomposity in her passing out examinations and had never for a moment considered allowing things to slide. 'It is not permitted for other persons to answer on behalf of the suitcase owner.'

'Then we could be here some time,' said Mrs Caldicot politely.

'And what's this?' demanded the customs officer, holding up a tin of apricot slices.

'That would probably be a tin of apricot slices,' said Mrs Caldicot. She bent down and looked at the tin. 'Freshly picked apricots, served in their own juice with no added sugar. They appear to have been grown in Uzbekistan. There's a recipe on the label for making an apricot tart.'

The customs officer picked out more tins and placed them on the counter beside Miss Nightingale's suitcase.

There were nine tins of mulligatawny soup, five tins of apricot slices in their own juice, none of them with any added sugar, and four tins of the very best Portuguese pilchards. It was now abundantly clear why Miss Nightingale's suitcase was so heavy.

'Do you have an export licence for these items?' asked the customs officer.

'They are for Miss Nightingale's own consumption,' explained Mrs Caldicot. Miss Nightingale was looking confused and rather upset. She didn't understand why this strange woman was unpacking her suitcase and examining her tins.

'Where are you going?' demanded the customs officer.

'To Paris,' replied Mrs Caldicot. 'Eventually,' she added, after a pause.

'For how long?'

'Three nights.'

'And what are these?' asked the customs officer, taking several packets out of the suitcase.

'They appear to be packets of biscuits,' replied Mrs Caldicot, who was a little annoyed by the customs officer's stupid questions. She peered more closely at the packets the customs person was holding. 'In fact I'm pretty sure that they are packets of biscuits. The packet with the words 'custard cream' on the sides will probably contain custard creams.' She examined the packets even more closely. 'Sadly, judging by the state of the packaging, they look as if they have probably become broken biscuits.'

There were seven packets of biscuits. All had been crushed.

'And all these are also for your consumption?' the customs officer asked Miss Nightingale.

Miss Nightingale looked at Mrs Caldicot.

'Yes,' said Mrs Caldicot, nodding at Miss Nightingale.

'Yes,' replied Miss Nightingale, nodding back at Mrs Caldicot.

Eleven minutes later, the suitcase was empty and half of the contents were spread out over the customs officer's counter. The rest of the contents were spread over a spare table which the officer had had to fetch in order to carry the overflow.

There were, in addition to the tinned foods and the biscuits and all the clothes which Mrs Caldicot had placed in the suitcase, three long playing records, two large packets of bird seed, a snow globe containing a model of Big Ben, a rag doll with an arm missing, a telephone directory dated 1998 and covering the L-K section of the population of London, a pair of wooden book ends in an art deco style, an unopened packet of vacuum cleaner bags, a half used roll of wallpaper (chintz pattern), a brand new roll of wallpaper (blue birds and butterflies against a background of cherry tree blossom), a remote control device for a television set, a spare inner tube for a bicycle, a vacuum attachment used for sucking crumbs from sofas and armchairs, and a tin of shaving foam.

'Ah, there it is!' said Mrs Caldicot spotting the remote control device for the television set. 'We've been looking for that for weeks.' She picked up the remote control and popped it into her handbag. It would, she thought and said out loud, be nice to find a different channel on the television.

'Put that back!' ordered the customs officer. 'It is not allowed for civilians to interfere with the functionality of customs officers.' She, like all her colleagues, was well aware that one of their number had been fired for laughing at a traveller's pleasantry. 'Service with a scowl' was thus their motto.

Mrs Caldicot took the remote control out of her bag and put it back on the counter. She was beginning to wish they had spent their lottery winnings on a new television set. Or a short holiday in the Lake District or Lyme Regis. Anywhere which didn't require passing through customs would have been fine.

At the same time, at another counter a few feet away, Mr Hewitt was trying to explain what a dibber was, why he had one in his suitcase and why it was necessary for him to take it to Paris.

'It's for making holes in the ground,' he explained. 'You push one end into the soil and then you drop in your seed. The Americans call it a dibble.'

The customs officer stared at him disbelievingly.

'When you've popped your seed in the hole you cover it up with soil, water it and wait for it to grow,' finished Mr Hewitt, using his hands to add to his explanation.

The customs man, who was from an East European nation where dibbers are about as commonplace as battery powered nose hair clippers, looked at the wooden dibber and then at Mr Hewitt. Obviously not a gardener, he was clearly not convinced by Mr Hewitt's explanation.

'OK,' said Mr Hewitt, with a weary sigh. 'It's a 19th century sex toy. They didn't have batteries in those days.'

'Ah,' said the customs man, with a sniff. He was much happier with this explanation. He firmly believed that all travellers to the continent were perverts, and he expected to be shocked. Mr Hewitt's false confession had comforted and reassured him. He picked the dibber up by the handle, being careful not to allow his gloved hands to come into contact with the business end of the device, and placed it back in Mr Hewitt's suitcase, alongside the hand-fork and the trowel. He didn't ask what the fork and trowel were for and did not seem excited by their presence.

Meanwhile, the customs officer who was dealing with the contents of Miss Nightingale's suitcase was still looking very confused. It was the first time she had seen anyone travelling with such an eclectic collection of items in their luggage and she wasn't sure whether there were any special procedures to be followed. For a moment she considered calling for a supervisor but then she looked at Miss Nightingale and decided not to bother.

'You can repack the case,' she said with an imperious wave of a hand.

'You can repack the case, thank you,' suggested Mrs Caldicot, politely.

The customs officer glowered at her.

Mrs Caldicot, who refused to be intimidated, glowered back. 'In three hours,' she thought, 'you will still be here going through people's dirty underwear whereas I could be sitting in a Parisian café sipping a glass of red wine and nibbling on a croissant.'

Momentarily, she felt guilty for thinking this. And then she realised that the thought made her feel much better and they can't (yet) lock you up for what you're thinking so she didn't feel quite so guilty after all.

'A 'thank you' would be very nice,' explained Mrs Caldicot.

'You may repack your case, thank you,' said the customs officer sourly. She managed to pronounce the final two words in a way that made it clear that she didn't mean them. But Miss Nightingale didn't notice and Mrs Caldicot no longer cared.

The customs officer then stood and watched as Mrs Caldicot attempted, in vain, to repack the suitcase. Without the help of Mrs Peterborough's ample proportions it was quite impossible to close the case. Miss Nightingale looked around, spotted her friend and beckoned her over.

'Do you need my bum?' said Mrs Peterborough cheerily.

Miss Nightingale nodded.

Mrs Peterborough pulled over a chair which she used to enable her to climb up onto the table and then onto Miss Nightingale's suitcase.

The table, which was standard government-issue, was not built to carry both a large, heavily laden suitcase and a large and heavily laden Mrs Peterborough and the inevitable result was that the suitcase, its contents, Mrs Peterborough and the broken table were spread across the floor. Instantly, the sour faced indigestion sufferer had her hands in front of her face and was screaming hysterically.

In complete contrast, Miss Nightingale and Mrs Peterborough were laughing. They thought it very funny. They always laughed at the same thing.

Mrs Caldicot could not help thinking that if it is true, as it is commonly said to be the case, that great minds think alike then Miss Nightingale and Mrs Peterborough must be blessed with great minds for there was no doubt that they thought alike very often.

The suitcase, its hinges broken, was now quite useless for its original purpose.

'Does anyone have a few spare plastic bags?' Mrs Caldicot asked, talking to the rest of her group and ignoring the customs officer who was having her own private but rather institutionalised version of hysterics.

Miss Nightingale picked up a bundle of her now temporarily homeless finery and, having looked around and realised that there was nowhere else to put it, wisely started to put on as many of her clothes as she could.

Within two minutes she was wearing three coats, four scarves and a variety hats. The hats were all of the woolly variety and she wisely made sure that the bright red one with the two dangly bobbles was put on top of the others.

'You look as if you've put on a lot of weight!' said Mrs Peterborough. 'You remind me of someone...'

Miss Nightingale puffed out her cheeks and held her arms out at her sides.

'I know who it is you remind me of...the Michelin Man!' cried Mrs Peterborough.

'The Michelin Woman!' agreed Miss Nightingale.

They both started to laugh again.

For a few years prior to his wartime experiences with the RAF's Bomber Command, Mr Livingstone, had been a boy scout, and he was therefore always prepared for any eventuality short of a tax inspection or a nuclear war. He therefore duly produced a fistful of plastic bags from a jacket pocket. They were flimsy bags, the sort of semi-useless artefacts sold for 5 pence each to supermarket customers, but they were the only bags available and so they were definitely better than nothing. Mr Livingstone handed half of the bags to Mrs Caldicot and kept the other half himself. Together they crammed Miss Nightingale's belongings into the plastic bags.

‘Would you please accept these with our compliments?’ Mrs Caldicot asked the customs officer, pointing to the four tins of Mulligatawny, the two tins of pilchards, the packets of broken biscuits and the assorted bundle of long playing records. (A symphony by Mahler, an original cast recording of *The King and I*, a collection of military band tunes and a recording of Des O’Connor’s greatest hits). It had not been possible to squeeze these back into the available plastic bags.

‘I’m not allowed to accept gifts,’ said the customs officer coldly. She had been released into the public domain with a few essential parts missing and had not yet worked out how to respond to situations which did not fit into the customs officer’s handbook, but she looked carefully at the tins. ‘And anyway I can’t eat pilchards. They’re the same thing as sardines aren’t they? I come out in a rash if I so much as look at a sardine.’

‘Then just pop them into the rubbish,’ said Mrs Caldicot sweetly. ‘We don’t seem to have room for them.’

‘And they give me terrible indigestion,’ added the customs officer. She flicked through the LPs and picked out the one by Des O’Connor. ‘Maybe just this…’

But as they moved away, Miss Nightingale turned back and grabbed everything that had not been packed into the plastic bags. She stuffed the broken biscuits and the tinned food into her coat pockets and tucked the long playing records under her arm. She also grabbed the Des O’Connor album.

The sour faced woman, who had decided to take the Des O’Connor album and who thought she might be able to cope with the Mulligatawny soup and would possibly be able to use the broken biscuits in a trifle, was so disappointed that she looked even more sour faced.

‘What about this broken suitcase?’ demanded the sour faced woman who had the face which reminded Mrs Caldicot of a horse’s behind. ‘Aren’t you taking it with you?’

Mrs Caldicot turned back. ‘Oh, you may keep that,’ she said sweetly. ‘Put it into the recycling.’

They then all showed their passports to a glum and bored looking Frenchman who had obviously done something bad in a previous life for he was now condemned to sitting in a plastic cubicle scowling and inspecting passports, and then, finally, they were through to the lounge where approximately half a million other travellers were awaiting their trains to the continent.

Oscar Wilde once said that 'it is a terrible thing to part from people one has known a very short time' but, as always, the dear soul, Oscar, was more concerned with the sound of what he said than with the sense of it. Mrs Caldicot and her chums were delighted to leave the customs folk behind. And they left without looking back or suffering any pangs of nostalgia.

They had three minutes to spare before the train departed and they hurried to join the queue. There were no trolleys available so Ruth and Mrs Roberts each had to carry or drag two large suitcases and several heavy looking shoulder bags.

'Do you think this counts as exercise?' asked Ruth, who was struggling for breath and perspiring profusely.

'Oh yes, definitely,' said Mrs Roberts who was in an equally bad state.

'I'm so pleased they didn't open my suitcase,' said Mrs Torridge, who was behind them in the queue. Her suitcase was on wheels but one of the wheels was slightly wonky and instead of following her like an obedient dog, the suitcase weaved from side to side as though it had several gins too many.

'I agree,' said Mrs Caldicot, who was also laden with bags and suitcases. 'I breathed a sigh of relief when mine was allowed through unopened.'

'Mr Torridge would have hated to be disturbed,' said Mrs Torridge. 'He was never a good traveller.'

Mrs Caldicot turned and looked at her and a cold shiver ran down her spine. Mrs Torridge had been a widow for fifteen years.

'Did Mr Torridge travel a good deal?' asked Mrs Caldicot, trying not to think what she had started to think.

'Oh no,' said Mrs Torridge, emphatically. 'Mr Torridge never went abroad. He didn't approve of foreign parts. But he didn't much like travelling in Britain either.'

'So,' said Mrs Caldicot, hesitantly, and not really wanting to hear the explanation that she felt sure was coming. 'What did you mean about him hating to be disturbed?'

'If they'd opened my suitcase,' explained Mrs Torridge. 'One of those horrible people might have taken him out and shaken him.

They might have even opened his lid.' She shuddered. 'He would have hated to have had his lid opened.'

Mrs Caldicot swallowed hard and made a real effort. 'Mr Torridge is in your suitcase?' She deliberately spoke very quietly partly so as not to alarm anyone else and partly to stop herself from screaming.

'Oh yes, I decided I couldn't travel without him.'

And then Mrs Caldicot remembered that Mrs Torridge kept her late husband in a coffee tin in her bedroom. Or, to be more accurate, she kept his ashes in the tin.

'You've brought Mr Torridge's ashes with you?' whispered Mrs Caldicot.

'Oh yes,' said Mrs Torridge as though it were the most sensible thing in the world; as though she had admitted to bringing with her a small alarm clock or a pair of slippers, for example. 'But it was a difficult decision. On the one hand I know he didn't like travelling when he was here with us in body. But on the other hand I've never been parted from him and I couldn't bear to leave him behind. In the end I thought he wouldn't mind me bringing him to Paris with me. I thought it would be a sort of second honeymoon.'

Mrs Caldicot closed her eyes and muttered a silent prayer of thanks that Mrs Torridge's case had passed through customs without being opened. She idly wondered if the passport man would have expected Mr Torridge's ashes to be accompanied by a suitably incinerated copy of his passport.

'We went to Torquay on our first honeymoon,' said Mrs Torridge. 'Mr Torridge liked Torquay. We stayed there for a whole week in a boarding house just two miles from the sea.' She smiled, remembering happy days in the Devon sunshine. 'Mr Torridge bought a fishing line and spent most days trying to catch mackerel. I sat beside him and watched. It was very romantic.' She paused, still thinking, still remembering. 'He never caught anything but he bought two from a man who'd been on one of those little boats and our landlady cooked them for our supper. Very nice they were too, but a little too bony for my taste.' There were tears in Mrs Torridge's eyes as she remembered a long ago mackerel supper and a husband who was no more.

Mrs Caldicot put her arm as far around Mrs Torridge as it would go and gave her a comforting squeeze. It occurred to her that with

Mr Torridge with them they were a party of 14 rather than 13. Mrs Caldicot was not a superstitious woman but it did seem that the presence of the additional member might not be a bad idea.

Struggling with their many suitcases, Mr Livingstone's instruments and Miss Nightingale's vast array of bulging plastic bags, they eventually boarded the train and settled in their seats. Mrs Caldicot could hardly believe it but they were, at last, off on their Paris adventure.

Chapter Nine

As their train went through the Channel Tunnel, Miss Nightingale celebrated the occasion by passing around the contents of the packets of broken biscuits which she'd stuffed in her pockets. The excitement of passing through Customs had long been forgotten by them all.

'This is the high life,' said Mr Roxdale, stuffing the crumbly remains of a badly battered custard cream into his mouth and lying back in his seat.

Mr Hewitt, who had managed to open one of Miss Nightingale's tins of apricot slices with the tin opening gadget on his Swiss Army penknife (which had, in all the excitement, slipped through the customs checks) pierced an apricot slice with the blade of the knife, popped the piece of fruit into his mouth and agreed with him. He then pierced another apricot slice and handed it to Mr Twist who was sitting in the seat next to him.

Mr Livingstone took his flute out of its case and minutes later those members of the party who weren't eating were singing the first of a fine variety of music hall songs.

Mr Livingstone liked music hall songs. He liked the tunes, he liked the words and he liked the jolly, having a good time sort of atmosphere they engendered.

Together they sang 'I'm Henry the Eighth', 'Burlington Bertie from Bow', 'Nellie Dean', 'Never Let Your Braces Dangle', 'Old Bull and Bush' and 'A Little Bit of Cucumber'. Miss Nightingale sang a solo version of Marie Lloyd's 'The Coster Girl in Paris' and Mrs Roberts surprised everyone by singing 'Has Anybody Here Seen Kelly?'. They sang 'Boiled Beef and Carrots' and 'I Do Like to Be Beside the Seaside'. Within ten minutes everyone in the carriage was singing along. Younger travellers who didn't know the words hummed or just made what they thought were appropriate da de da type noises.

Everyone had what used to be called a jolly good time (and would probably now be known as an 'interesting inter-generational experience') and Mrs Caldicot, who was very proud of her friends, had to wipe away a tear or two of happiness.

A couple of hours later the train slowed and eased into the Gare du Nord railway station in northern Paris.

'Can't we go round again?' shouted a young man with green hair. His friends, who had never enjoyed a journey so much, laughed and cheered.

Ruth smiled. She was very happy. Two young men had asked her for her telephone number and she felt sure that a little fellow with a toothbrush moustache and a glint in his eye had pinched her bottom. The train had jolted while she was coming back from the loo and it was, of course, possible that she might have simply bumped into the edge of a table or a piece of luggage. But the little fellow, who was too old and too small for her to fancy, and whom she felt was certainly foreign and probably French, had winked at her. She had glowered at him, though in a friendly, encouraging sort of way, and he had winked again.

And since you couldn't really count being on a train as being abroad they hadn't really arrived in France yet. She couldn't wait to send a text to her best friend Denise to let her know what had happened.

Chapter Ten

It was quite probably true that the coach driver who met them at the Gare du Nord, who helped load their bags into the bowels of his rather aged and battered vehicle and who then drove them to their hotel, was, technically speaking, bilingual as advertised.

Whatever his French was like, he was not exactly fluent in the English language but, as Mrs Roberts later pointed out, it was perfectly possible that he really was bilingual but that neither of his mastered languages was English.

'Maybe his two chosen languages are Swedish and Romanian,' she suggested. 'That would make him bilingual.'

'My name is Marc,' the driver announced with a broad smile, when they had all boarded the coach and settled into their seats. He had clearly practised this phrase many times for he made the announcement loudly, clearly and confidently. Mrs Caldicot and her party were impressed.

But, sadly, that was about the extent of Marc's English.

'How far is it to the hotel?' asked Mrs Caldicot, as the coach eased out into heavy traffic.

'L'Hotel est magnifique!' replied Marc ignoring the question because he hadn't understood it. 'Il y a un ascenseur.'

'What did he say?' asked Mrs Caldicot, turning round to see if anyone could help translate. Mrs Caldicot's French was limited in scope and not all social situations can be dealt with effectively with 'Un café, s'il vous plait.'

'He said something about a Russian called Ilya,' said Mr Livingstone confidently. He thought for a moment. 'Maybe this Ilya is the manager,' he suggested.

'He said that the hotel is magnificent and that there is a lift,' said Mr Williams softly.

'Yes, exactly, that's what I thought he said,' agreed Mr Livingstone who was beginning to suspect that perhaps his French was a little rustier than he had thought.

Mrs Caldicot thanked them both.

'L'hotel dispose de soixante seize chambres toutes avec salle de bain,' said Marc, swerving to avoid a taxi which had suddenly stopped in the middle of the road.

Marc, the driver, seemed determined to prove that even if he did not speak much English, he could definitely speak some French.

He was so keen to tell them about the hotel that he seemed to have forgotten that he was driving a coach, and threw the large vehicle around as if it were a high performance rally car and he a competition driver fighting for vital points in the World Rally Championship.

It seemed to Mrs Caldicot that the traffic was less regulated in France than in England and it was certainly faster, more thrilling, and more dangerous. The drivers seemed to do a good deal more gesticulating and it was all very noisy too; with a good deal of horn blowing.

It was not, thought Mrs Caldicot, a place for timid drivers.

'I think he said something about the hotel having a girl called Sally de something who empties lots of chamber pots,' said Mr Livingstone, translating the driver's last remarks. He paused and thought for a while. 'I couldn't quite make out the girl's name. But I seem to remember that they don't think they have proper toilets in France. They squat down and use a sort of hole in the ground.'

'If the toilet is just a hole in the ground what do you do if you're on the top floor of a tall building?' asked Mr Hewitt.

'The hotel has 76 bedrooms, all with private bathrooms,' murmured Mr Williams, translating what the driver had said and speaking before Mr Livingstone could answer this perfectly sensible question.

'Maybe a long pipe?' suggested Mr Livingstone who was still fascinated by the idea of a top floor toilet which connected to a hole in the ground. 'But what if it backed up? That would be a hell of a problem wouldn't it?'

'I think we'll find that the hotel has proper lavatories,' whispered Mr Williams.

The driver slammed on his brakes as a cyclist rode in front of him. He swerved around the cyclist and then accelerated furiously. He sounded his horn, shouted something which was almost certainly not complimentary, changed gear, waved a fist at the cyclist and lit a cigarette. He seemed to manage to do all these things at the same time. Mrs Caldicot noticed with horror that he appeared to be steering the coach with his knees. A delivery van hurtled in front of the coach, missing it by inches or, since they were now in France, by centimetres.

'I don't think I need to translate that,' said Mr Williams dryly. 'And unless he knows the cyclist and his parents I don't see how he could know all that anyway.'

Ten minutes later, the coach slid to a tyre screaming halt outside a nondescript grey building which should have had the word 'Hotel' in neon lights above the door. However, there was something wrong with the light and the H was not lit. The four remaining letters blazed away with glorious defiance. OTEL they cried proudly.

Marc the coach driver had double parked and seemed unaware that he was now completely blocking the narrow street.

'Oh look!' said Ruth excitedly. 'The French use almost the same word as we do – but they leave off the H.'

'It doesn't look very grand,' whispered Mrs Roberts, who sounded rather disappointed.

A motorist, who had been waiting behind the coach for nearly five seconds, started to press his horn.

'I'm sure it's very nice inside,' said Mrs Caldicot. 'And we aren't going to spend much time looking at the outside, are we?'

'True!' laughed Mrs Roberts.

A second motorist, now joining the young queue behind the coach, put his hand on his horn button. A delivery van driver joined the queue and did the same. The horns all had their own individual tones. Marc leant out of his window and glowered at them all. He then waved a single, nicotine stained finger in their general direction. Somehow, the horn blowing seemed to increase in intensity. One of the drivers wound down his window and shouted something which was probably abusive.

'Welcome to the best 'otel in Paris!' said a short man who wore a green jacket, green trousers and a green peaked hat. The jacket, trousers and hat were all decorated with yellow piping and had been made for a taller man with a larger head. The man wearing them looked to be in his 20s.

'Are you the porter?' asked Mrs Caldicot.

'I am Raphael, the hotel doorman,' said the short man. 'I speak perfect English. Anything you wants you have only to be asking yourself from me. I can tell you everything for which you have needs. Welcome to the 'otel.' He had to shout to make himself heard above the sound of the horn blowing. He did not seem surprised or in any way put out by this.

'Can you help us with our luggage?' asked Mrs Caldicot, not unreasonably.

'I do not do the luggages,' said Raphael, rather indignantly. 'I am the doorman. If I disappear into the hotel with bags I cannot be also the doorman, is not? If someone arrives and I am there not here will be an absence of doorman and the 'otel manager he will not be pleased. I will lose my job and have to give back my uniform. There are very few jobs of this type in Paris.' He moved closer to Mrs Caldicot and lowered his voice. 'I can, however, arrange for you everything you may be needing while you are enjoying your stay in Paris. I can fix for you the taxis, the nightclubs, the restaurants, the companions for the evening…' He allowed the sentence to trail off.

Mrs Caldicot was surprised at Raphael's refusal to help with the bags. He was, she thought, perhaps not the best choice as a hotel doorman. But, on the other hand, maybe it was not easy to find a man prepared to wear an ill-fitting green uniform with yellow piping and to stand on a doorstep all day long.

And when she thought about it, she was unable to counter his seemingly solid piece of logic. If you have a man who is hired as a doorman then you would expect him to stay by the door. Moreover, she was slightly unnerved by Raphael's stern prediction about what would happen if he carried their cases into the hotel. She didn't want the poor fellow to lose his job.

And so, Mrs Caldicot, anxious to move herself, her companions and their luggage out of the coach and away from the pavement before the traffic jam, and the noise which the constituent parts were making, attracted the attention of the police, decided that they had all better carry their own luggage into the hotel.

Carrying her own suitcase, her handbag, and six of Miss Nightingale's plastic bags, Mrs Caldicot led the way into the hotel. She was glad to get away from the cacophony outside. The others, most of them equally burdened, followed her faithfully. The doorman, who was definitely not a porter, stood aside so that they could more easily make their way into the 'otel.

Inside, the narrow reception hall led up to a horse-shoe shaped, plastic looking reception desk, behind which there stood a young woman who was wearing a white blouse and a smart blue blazer which had gold buttons and an impressive looking badge on the breast pocket. The badge told anyone who dared to look close enough that her name was Nathalie and that she was the 'receptionniste'. Given her situation and the name badge, it seemed reasonable to assume that she was the hotel receptionist. Whatever else she was wearing was, together with the other half of her body, hidden behind the reception desk. Throughout the reception area, a powerful smell of furniture polish was fighting a battle with a pungent disinfectant. The aroma of the receptionist's perfume had lost the battle and apparently resigned itself to a walk on part as an insignificant extra.

The reception looked to be in her twenties but could, Mrs Caldicot thought, have been older than that. Mrs Caldicot thought she looked a nice, young girl and she was right about this.

The receptionist was a gentle, kind, sensitive creature who never went to the cinema without two packets of paper handkerchiefs in her handbag. She enjoyed a good weep and liked to categorise films according to their capacity to induce tears. So, therefore, a 'good' film would require three tissues whereas an excellent one would require at least five. She had, fortuitously, a great fondness for old people. Her grandmother (now long promoted to the Great Knitting Academy in the sky but the spitting image of Mrs Torridge) still had a place in her heart and she was never happier than when she was welcoming a party of aged tourists to the hotel. Old people were, in her experience, far less likely to get drunk, turn rowdy or set off the fire extinguishers.

To the left of the reception desk there was a staircase and to the right there was something which looked like a small cupboard but which, on closer examination, turned out to be the hotel lift. A pile of plastic stacking chairs had been left to the left of the lift doors, rather restricting ingress and egress. The whole area had clearly been freshly and extensively redecorated at some point in its life, though this had probably been a couple of decades earlier and whoever it was who had planned the renovations had been fond of brown

Formica and had purchased a considerable quantity of the stuff, clearly with some enthusiasm.

The carpet, which was red with a fleus de lys pattern in gold, had doubtless been regarded with some pride when it had been lain and if there had been any guarantees about its hard wearing nature, the owners of the hotel might now be remembering any such promises with a certain amount of chagrin for there were bare patches on those areas of carpet most traversed by guests and staff.

Mrs Caldicot was reminded that Jenkins had told her that the Parisians don't much care whether their homes need a lick of paint, and don't give a fig if their cars are well decorated with dents and scratches, but they do like to present themselves as though they never know when they might need to attend a job interview or a court hearing.

'You are welcoming by the 'otel!' said the receptionist with a smile that would have filled a television presenter with envy. The receptionist's teeth were so white that Mrs Caldicot felt she would need dark glasses if she had to talk to the girl for long. 'My name is Hortense and I am speaking perfectly the English so you will ask me for any questions. We were hoped that you were having a great journey and that Marc has been bringing you here safely.'

'Oh yes, thank you,' said Mrs Caldicot, who was still shaking from the coach ride from the station and to be honest still rather cross that the man at the door, in the uniform, had steadfastly declined to help them carry their bags into the hotel. 'We got here quite safely, thank you very much.'

She thought, but did not say, that this was probably more a result of the silent prayer she had murmured than of the driver's skills.

'You will be signing the papers,' said the receptionist. She pushed a card and a form across the counter and held out a pen. Mrs Caldicot put down some of her bags, took the pen and signed her name twice.

'Everyone needs to be signing,' said the receptionist. 'There are much papers.' She raised her eyes towards the ceiling in that way people do when they are making clear that they think the world to be controlled by buffoons. 'Always so much papers!'

Mrs Caldicot looked behind her. The hall and reception area were now full of people and bags. 'Can't I sign for everyone?' she asked.

The receptionist smiled, looked from side to side as though to make sure that no one was looking, and pushed a pile of forms across the counter. 'It will be more faster,' she whispered.

Mrs Caldicot scribbled her signature on all the cards and pieces of paper and then pushed them back towards the receptionist.

'What do you have to do with all those?' asked Mrs Caldicot, pointing to the sheaf of papers and cards. 'What happens to them?'

'I put them in here,' said the receptionist. She shuffled the pieces of paper and cards which Mrs Caldicot had signed so that they looked reasonably neat and then dropped them onto the top of a pile of similar forms and cards which filled a metal filing tray. 'And when that is full and can take no more I must putting all of them into there.' She pointed to a large cardboard box on the floor behind her.

'And when the box is full?'

'It goes down into the cellars for storage,' said the receptionist. 'It is too heavy for me so I have to speak nicely to one of the waiters or to Raphael. You have met Raphael I think?'

'Oh yes,' agreed Mrs Caldicot.

The receptionist pulled the corners of her mouth down and again rolled her eyes upwards. She leant forwards a little. 'You must I think be careful of him,' she said. 'He likes very much the fees and commissions. You understand? He receives money, how is the phrase, the backbribe?'

'Backhander,' said Mrs Caldicot. 'We say 'backhander'.'

'Ah yes. That is correct. He receives the 'backhanders' from everyone – ten euros here, twenty euros there, one hundred euros sometimes. Oh la la! He must be very rich.'

'Oh yes,' said Mrs Caldicot. 'I think I understand.' She definitely liked the receptionist.

The receptionist pointed to a doorway. 'The reception committee is remaining for you all in the 'otel lounge,' said the receptionist. 'You will be filled with pleasure to be going through there. The committee has been arranging for the 'otel to be assembling champagne and small biscuits with on them little knobs of cheese. You will very much be admiring our varieties of French knobs we have provided for your delights.'

'Goodness, how kind,' said Mrs Caldicot, resisting the temptation to point out that in England it is only usually butter which is served up as knobs. She picked up the bags she had put down and, with some difficulty, managed to open the heavy door which the receptionist had indicated.

Mrs Roberts, Ruth and the rest of the party bravely followed her into the unknown, all still carrying their bags and cases. Only Mrs Caldicot knew that they were about to be regaled with unspecified quantities of champagne and little biscuits decorated with knobs of French cheeses. The rest were simply, blindly and faithfully following Mrs Caldicot.

Chapter Eleven

The room which Mrs Caldicot entered was smaller than she had expected and it seemed, pretty well packed with people.

There were about a dozen in there, each one holding a flute of champagne, and as Mrs Caldicot and the others entered the room they raised the glasses and shouted 'Welcome!' and though they tried to do it in unison they did not manage this very well and so the cry was rather ragged and less impressive than it might have been.

A waiter, who had one of those hairstyles favoured by monks which involve a fringe of hair and a large, central bald patch, and who was carrying a large, silver tray full of glasses filled with champagne, approached her. A white, plastic name tag pinned to his jacket announced that his name was 'Pierre'. It was clear that Mrs Caldicot, and the others, were each expected to take a glass. Behind him, a younger waiter, whose name badge told the world that his name was 'Jean-Jacques', was also offering a tray but his tray was full of assorted French nibbly things.

'This is very nice of the hotel,' whispered Mrs Caldicot to Mrs Roberts, as they put down their bags and each took a glass of the champagne. 'Who do you think all these people are? Do you think they all work here? I wonder if they do this for all their guests?'

'We are full of proudness to welcoming you to Paris for this your first timing!' said a small, middle-aged man in a purple suit which looked as though it had been made out of a very nice piece of velour curtain material. He was wearing a lilac shirt and a rather large, bright yellow bow tie and a cardboard name badge attached to his jacket announced to the world, or at least to any part of it that might be interested, that his name was Olivier.

'I am Olivier,' announced the man, thereby proving that he was at least wearing the right jacket and the correct name badge. He made this announcement as though he were certain that they would know this anyway, but that he felt it only polite of him to pretend that they didn't recognise him. Television personalities do it all the time;

introducing themselves by name even when they would be mortified if the person to whom they were introducing themselves didn't already know precisely who they were. It is their way of letting the world know that they haven't been changed by their success but are still the same, modest folk they were before they became famous.

'I am the President du Conseil,' he announced, 'and I am satisfied to be the representative of the City of Paris for this red-letter evening.'

He moved forwards and kissed Mrs Caldicot three times. He kissed her right cheek, then her left cheek and then, as though he wasn't sure he'd done it right the first time, kissed her right cheek again. These were not media mwah mwah air kisses, missing the skin by inches. These were resounding full contact kisses. Olivier had unusually rubbery, wet lips and Mrs Caldicot really wanted to take out her handkerchief and wipe her face but she didn't think it would be considered proper etiquette. It suddenly occurred to her that she did not think that the late, and now unlamented, Mr Caldicot had kissed her so many times in his entire life.

'Oh, that's very nice,' Mrs Caldicot said, bravely leaving her handkerchief in her handbag and belatedly backing away slightly from the flurry of unexpected osculatory activity. 'Congratulations,' she murmured not quite knowing what to say but knowing that 'Congratulations' generally goes down well when someone has told you something that doesn't involve a bereavement, details of a newly diagnosed serious illness or a serious financial loss of any kind.

'Since you are guests in our country, it is insisted that we is speaking English to you,' said Olivier when he had completed his rather slobbery welcome. 'It is very good for you to be of meeting us after so many emailings together. We can shoot the breeze in cahoots, yes?'

Mrs Caldicot wondered if she was supposed to kiss Olivier back but before she could decide, she realised that she was too late because Olivier had already moved on to kiss Mrs Roberts. Right cheek, left cheek, right cheek. Mrs Roberts blushed heavily and made a strange fluttering motion with her hands as though vaguely trying to fight off these not entirely unwelcome attentions. Truly, she did not mind the attention. There had been no Mr Roberts for some years and she was a keen follower of the style of romantic fiction popularised by Georgette Heyer. She patted her hair as though anxious to make sure that it had not been disturbed by the encounter.

'I am speaking English of excellence so we speak the langue together,' said Olivier, with what Mrs Caldicot, innocent of the French character, thought was more than enough self-assurance for everyone in the room.

'That's lovely,' said Mrs Caldicot. 'Your English is perfect.'

Ruth, who was next in the firing line, had yet to be kissed but was already blushing bright red and was glad she hadn't yet had chance to send a text to Denise. Now she could tell her that although she'd been in Paris no more than fifteen minutes she had already been kissed three times. She wouldn't bother to mention that the three kisses had all come from the same man and there was certainly no need to mention that he had been a diminutive, middle aged man in a purple suit and a bright yellow bow tie. She wondered how much shorter than her the man was. Nine inches? Six inches? No, probably less than that. She wondered if French men were all small. And did they all like tall women? She looked around the room and caught the eye of the younger waiter. He smiled at her and she blushed an even deeper red. He had a small, gold earring in his left ear lobe and a tattoo on his neck. She felt the blush moving down her neck towards her chest and was glad that her blue anorak was still zipped up to her throat. She wondered if the waiters would also be kissing everybody. She suddenly remembered that she must mention the man on the train who had almost certainly pinched her bottom. She didn't think there was any need to mention the 'almost certainly'.

A woman in a bright blue hat shaped like a flower pot was now kissing Mrs Caldicot's cheeks (right cheek, left cheek, right cheek) and Mrs Caldicot found herself wondering whether all this kissing was really hygienic. If she'd known, she thought, she would have given her face an extra wash before they'd left home that morning. And she'd certainly give her face a double wash when she finally reached the sanctuary of her hotel room.

'I know this,' said Olivier, modestly brushing aside the unnecessary compliment with a casual but rather flamboyant wave of the hand which was holding his champagne flute, showering the carpet with champagne as he did so. Mrs Caldicot thought he had probably had one or two drinks already and was about to turn philosophical. She wondered idly if he would then turn left into maudlin introspection and the inevitable tears, or turn right into aggression, staring eyes, jutting jaw and an urgent desire to 'knock someone's block into next week' (or the French equivalent).

He moved on to start kissing Mrs Torridge, who seemed to be next in line.

The other members of what appeared to be some sort of welcoming committee were now lining up behind him and Mrs Caldicot found herself being kissed for the fifth or sixth time. There was a man with a large beard in the queue and she hoped she wouldn't giggle if his beard tickled her. Ruth was trying to keep count of the number of times she had been kissed. She wondered whether or not to tell Denise about all the women who were kissing her. She didn't want people at home talking and getting the wrong impression. Some of the people Denise knew could be a bit gossipy at times. Still, the people kissing her were all foreign and she had read that they did things differently in foreign parts, particularly in France where, she understood, naughtiness had been invented, improved and served up to the rest of the world.

Meanwhile, Ruth was disappointed to see that the waiters were not doing any kissing.

Behind her, Mrs Caldicot heard Miss Nightingale giggling as someone kissed her. She would probably kiss them back, thought Mrs Caldicot. And it would probably be a full on lips kiss with slightly more saliva than is usually considered polite in osculatory circles. Some high-pitched giggling suggested to her that Miss Nightingale had indeed responded to the kissing in what would doubtless seem to the French to be an entirely inappropriate way.

When, finally, there was a temporary break in the kissing, Mrs Caldicot turned to Mrs Roberts, who was standing beside her. 'Who are these people? Have they made a mistake? Who do they think we are?'

'Oh dear,' said Mrs Roberts, who was blushing lightly, 'I didn't like to mention it but I think they've mistaken us for the 'Faversham Food and Fashion Fellowship for Fervent Francophiles.'

'The who? The what?'

Mrs Roberts pointed to a black peg board upon which someone had spelt out the words: 'Bienvenu a Favershamp Food and Fashion Fallowship pour Fervente Francophilles' in little, white, plastic letters. The spelling might have left a little to be desired but the sentiment was clear and wholesome.

'Why on earth would they mistake us for these people from Faversham?' asked Mrs Caldicot.

'Do you remember that when we made our booking, I told you that we'd been able to fix our tickets because another group had had to cancel their booking?'

'I do. They all had measles or ptomaine poisoning or something equally unpleasant.'

'Whatever they had they couldn't travel with it.'

'And they were from Faversham?'

'Faversham wasn't mentioned but I rather suspect that might be where they were from.'

'So we took the booking which was originally intended for the Faversham Food and Fashion Fellowship for Fervent Francophiles?'

'Indeed so.'

'And no one remembered to tell the French people that the Faversham Francophiles had cancelled and so they now think that we are them?'

'I think that must be what happened.'

'Oh dear me. What are we going to do?'

Mrs Caldicot's first thought was that they needed to get away from the reception party as soon as possible. She did not want the French people patronising her friends, or treating them with disrespect just because they were old and, in some cases, a little confused and bewildered by the curious ways of the world.

'I think it's probably rather too late to tell them their mistake,' said Mrs Roberts.

'So we should just have another glass of champagne and some of those little biscuits with the bits of cheese on them?'

'Knobs on,' said Mrs Roberts with a giggle. 'If Mr Livingstone and Mr Hewitt haven't eaten them all before we get there.'

Mrs Caldicot looked across the room and saw that Mr Livingstone and Mr Hewitt were busily scoffing small, savoury biscuits with cheese piled on top of them as though they were taking part in one of those eating competitions where the contestants must scoff as many meat pies or sausages as they can within a given time. Except, of course, that instead of scoffing meat pies or sausages they were munching their way through little biscuits piled high with cheese and doing so as though the continuation of the entente cordiale depended upon them.

Suddenly, they heard the unusually fortissimo sound of Mrs Peterborough's unmistakable voice. Mrs Peterborough had taken to reciting occasional limericks. These invariably delighted the audience. As a young woman, over half a century earlier, she had studied English Literature at Oxford University and although she had earned her living in haberdashery, she had aspired to be a poet. She had, indeed, published a number of poems in small magazines.

In recent weeks, she had adopted the limerick form as her chosen medium.

'I call this poem 'The Waiter' she said. She was speaking rather loudly, in what Mrs Caldicot called her 'limerick voice' and without delay she proceeded to recite her latest limerick.

A middle-aged waiter called Pierre
Had a hole where there should have been hair
He declared, with a smile,
'It's been gone for a while,
But I really can't say that I care.'

Mr Livingstone, who was a great fan of Mrs Peterborough's limericks, started to applaud. The other members of the British contingent joined in immediately. No one clapped with more enthusiasm than Miss Nightingale, the loyalist of loyal companions. And the French hosts, determined not to be outdone or to appear rude, also joined in. Mrs Caldicot couldn't help wondering what the French really thought.

Mrs Peterborough, proud as Punch, and twice as charming, beamed with delight.

Mrs Caldicot, who knew from past experience that Mrs Peterborough's limericks could sometimes be a trifle on the earthy side of socially acceptable, breathed a sigh of relief. She noticed that Olivier was sitting on the corner of a table with tears streaming down his face. He was nodding as though in agreement with someone about something. The champagne flute which he was holding in his right hand was empty.

'It is very wondrous for you to be having us here like we are,' said a very thin woman with high cheekbones and very short hair. She had a very high-pitched, whiny sort of voice which made her sound as though she were being strangled, though in a nice enough sort of way. She was wearing a cream trouser suit made out of silk and a pair of matching shoes which, Mrs Caldicot guessed, had probably cost as much as her own entire outfit. The woman's name tag bore the name 'Stephanie'.

'Thank you,' said Mrs Caldicot, who wasn't sure what to say but thought that a fairly vanillary 'thank you' wouldn't go far wrong.

'You are understanding me?'

'Oh yes,' said Mrs Caldicot. 'Your English is so good!'

'Yes, thank you,' said the thin woman, accepting the compliment without hesitation. 'You are right to say that, of course. I have learned for some years to become the fluency in the foreign languages. I am also uttering the Italian at this very moment.'

'Have you been to England at all?' asked Mrs Caldicot, speaking slowly and trying to enunciate clearly in the way that people are encouraged to do when communicating with foreigners.

'Ruefully not,' said Stephanie. 'It is shameful and flagitious.'

'Have you visited anywhere in Britain? Scotland? Wales? Northern Ireland?'

'I went visiting to Calais at one duration and could see your white cliffs of Dover across the French seas,' said Stephanie. 'Magnifique!' She turned up the smile a few watts and moved a little closer. 'I am hoping that bounteous English persons will invite me to their dwelling for a visit. Maybe I meet a nice, high Englishman who wipes me off my foot.'

'Oh yes that would be nice,' agreed Mrs Caldicot, trying to suppress the image of Stephanie being wiped off her foot by a kind Englishman. 'What is the name of your society?'

'The what are you saying?'

'What is the name of your organisation; the group of which you are a member?'

'We are being 'La Societe pour la promotion de Cuisine Francaise et de la Mode'. In English that is, I am thinking it is rendered as: 'The Society for the Promotion of French Food and Fashion'. I am the secretaire of the society and in my daytime busyness I am the femme responsible des relations publiques for Doris Guillain which is one of the big fashion homes here in Paris. You may have heard of it, yes?'

Mrs Caldicot gave her congratulations and, although she had never heard of Doris Guillain she naturally said she had. Whenever it was possible, Mrs Caldicot always liked to make people happy.

'Who was the lady who recited the poem?'

'That was Mrs Peterborough.'

'It was a poem by your Wilhelm Shakespeare, no? Or perhaps your William of Wordsworth? Maybe the good Lords Byron? Or, maybe, the great American known as Walt Whitman?'

'No, actually, I don't think it was any of those. I think it was a little something Mrs Peterborough made up on the spur of the moment.'

'She is a poet?' gasped Stephanie. 'She is being a famous poet in England, perhaps?'

'I don't know about famous,' began Mrs Caldicot. She thought for a while. What harm could it do? 'Well yes, indeed, I suppose she is quite a famous poet,' she agreed at last. 'As you can see, she is very popular.'

Stephanie thanked her and hurried off to join the small crowd which now surrounded Mrs Peterborough.

Even from a few yards away, Mrs Caldicot could hear Mrs Peterborough talking to a plump man in a very smart grey suit. He had fleshy lips, horn-rimmed spectacles and wore a grey, silk scarf draped around his neck.

She noticed that Olivier was now lying on the carpet. His eyes were shut and he appeared to be talking to himself.

'I was in haberdashery myself,' said Mrs Peterborough enthusiastically. 'My husband and I owned a shop which we ran together. In America, a haberdashery sells clothes for men. But in Britain, a haberdashery sells bits and pieces for sewing. Haberdashery isn't much of a business these days because women don't sew as much as they used to. But when we had our shop we were always busy. We sold thread and buttons and zips, those were our main items, but we also sold gloves and spare elastic straps for suspender belts. We sold lots of accessories of that type. I myself was considered quite an expert on buttons.'

And Mrs Caldicot listened in amazement as Mrs Peterborough proceeded to give the plump man in the grey suit a comprehensive account of the button business. Mrs Peterborough talked about wooden buttons, metal buttons, glass buttons, porcelain buttons, leather buttons and mother-of-pearl buttons. She talked knowledgeably about the history of buttons. She spoke about shank buttons, sew-through buttons, stud buttons and fabric buttons. It were as though all this material had been lost, tucked away in some dark recess of her mind, and now that it was released it just poured out. Mrs Caldicot listened in awe for this was a Mrs Peterborough she had never known before; a woman whose life had been packed with special knowledge and experience. It was quickly clear that what Mrs Peterborough didn't know about haberdashery wasn't worth knowing.

'My husband and I ran the business for years,' said Mrs Peterborough. 'But to be truthful it was the business running us rather than the other way around. In the end it killed him, poor lamb. He had a heart attack and died. I always thought it was the ribbons which killed him. People would come in wanting two yards or three yards or whatever of the pink half inch ribbon or the lilac three quarter inch ribbon and when we got to the end of the spool there would always be a little bit left over that no one ever wanted to buy. All those little bits of leftover ribbon worried him enormously. He used to say they were our lost profits.'

On Mrs Caldicot's other side, she could hear Mr Livingstone discussing famous French chefs such as August Escoffier, Marie-Antoine Careme and Raymond Oliver with a very small man in a white three piece suit who appeared to be enormously impressed. Mrs Caldicot found herself wondering how and why Mr Livingstone knew so much about French chefs. She didn't even know that he was interested in cooking in general or French cuisine in particular.

And when she heard Mrs Torridge chatting away about women's clothing fashions in the 1950s, Mrs Caldicot suddenly remembered that the frail and rather plump old lady who had fallen down without her walking frame had once been an important buyer for a major chain store.

Mrs Caldicot looked around at her friends and realised that so much had changed since she had first met them.

For one thing, they all seemed taller now.

They actually appeared to be at least a foot taller!

This was, of course, impossible.

It was not that they had actually grown.

But when she had first met them they had all been bent over, stooped under the burden of despair and hopelessness. They had been living pointless, oppressed lives: serving only to enrich those paid to look after them. Now, they were standing up like soldiers on parade. They had self-respect and it showed. It was, she thought to herself, amazing how the mind can change the shape and appearance of the body.

'It's easy to forget that old people have all done amazing things with their lives,' said Ruth, who was listening to Mrs Torridge with a good deal of astonishment and a great deal of awe.

'It is,' agreed Mrs Caldicot who was so proud of her friends that she had to wipe away a tear which had somehow managed to escape onto her cheek.

'I'm so used to her being old and a bit, you know, dotty, that I'd forgotten that she had been young once,' whispered Ruth.

'She was a very beautiful woman when she was young,' said Mrs Caldicot who had seen photographs of Mrs Torridge when she had been younger. 'And she was very bright. She was a high flyer long before women were allowed to become high flyers. Like the others she may not always be at her best these days, and she may be a trifle eccentric and a little wobbly occasionally, but it annoys me when older people aren't treated with the respect they deserve.'

The two of them looked around the room. Every member of her party had suddenly found themselves digging deep into their bank of memories. A long forgotten word here or there had triggered recollections and released knowledge that had been locked away for years; unused and apparently forgotten.

Their French hosts were, it seemed, quite entranced.

Mrs Caldicot vowed there and then that when they got back home she would make sure that her friends would all have every opportunity to recover and share their knowledge, their experience and their acquired wisdom.

A few yards away, Mr Williams was involved in what seemed to be a deep and meaningful conversation with a man and a woman. Mr Williams appeared to be speaking fluent French without any difficulty or hesitation.

Mrs Roberts, who did not speak any French, was standing nearby looking absolutely dumbfounded. Suddenly, she saw Mrs Caldicot and hurried over to her.

'Mr Williams is speaking perfect French!' she said. 'He's chatting to those French people in their own language.'

'Golly,' said Mrs Caldicot. 'He did say he knew some French but I didn't know he was fluent.'

Mrs Caldicot stood for a moment and watched him chatting away. Then she looked around the room. The champagne reception was a huge success. All her friends from England were now engaged in earnest conversations with their French hosts.

Even Miss Nightingale had found an excellent way to woo the natives. She had discovered several handfuls of biscuit crumbs in her pockets and was sharing out the crumbs as though they were fragments of Perigord black truffle; snuffled out of the ground that morning by a well-trained porcine detective. The packaging, the wrapping within which the biscuits had met their crushing defeat under the weight of Mrs Peterborough's ample buttocks, had long since been abandoned; crumpled and tossed neatly into a rubbish bin. Only the biscuit crumbs remained.

Olivier, who appeared to have recovered, was now tentatively tasting a thimble sized portion of well crushed custard cream and mangled Garibaldi remnants. He nodded appreciatively as he gratefully accepted a second helping of what he took to be a strange English delicacy. Olivier had never had much time for the English or the British (he was not entirely sure of the difference between 'English' and 'British' and if he had been at school and set one of those compare and contrast exercises which were so popular when he'd been a boy, he would have failed the task miserably) but he was warming to this particular selection of imports. 'These old folk look pretty threadbare,' he muttered to a colleague. 'But there is more to them than meets the eye.'

Mrs Caldicot worried for a moment that it might have seemed a little odd that Miss Nightingale's biscuit crumb delicacy should be served straight from the pocket but then realised that the French are not, of course, strangers to culinary oddities. This is, she realised, a race which had the idea of collecting snails from the garden, winkling them out of their shells and serving them up in garlic butter. And had then topped their own culinary eccentricity by wondering what a frog's legs would taste like if sautéed in a little of their ubiquitous garlic butter, baked in butter, parsley and lemon juice or dipped in a little egg mix and lightly battered.

Biscuit crumbs served straight from the pocket must seem positively mundane to the French.

'Lovely aren't they?' said Miss Nightingale, pouring more crushed biscuit into the Frenchman's cupped palm.

'This is an English delicacy?'

'Oh yes,' said Miss Nightingale enthusiastically. She started to laugh. She had a wonderful, infectious laugh that was so easy and genuine that it always made other people smile and want to laugh too. Within a minute, everyone around her was also laughing and, if asked, they would have doubtless admitted that although they did not know precisely why they were laughing they did know that they were having a jolly good time.

'Who would have thought it!' said Ruth, speaking softly, more to herself than to anyone else.

Ruth was a good and kind person; she had always been fond of the old people she helped care for, and she had, from the beginning, treated them with respect, somehow subconsciously aware of their innate right to dignity, but now she realised for the first time that although they might be a little unsteady from time to time (both mentally and physically) they had done many things with their lives and that dignity and respect were their right, earned and paid for, and not a charitable donation to be bestowed out of a sense of superiority or handed out, in a patronising way, like a bowl of soup and a piece of bread.

She now realised, for the first time in her life, that although the young often have a tendency to say a great deal without ever saying anything worth hearing, older citizens, although often reluctant to speak, do, when they eventually speak, invariably say something worth listening to.

The champagne reception finished only when the hotel receptionist appeared and explained that the staff needed to prepare the room for the next morning's breakfast.

Closing down the evening's event was not something which could be done quickly.

First, everyone had to kiss everyone else three times (right cheek, left cheek, right cheek) and then Mr Livingstone insisted that they all shake hands with one another, in a properly formal English way.

There were many promises to 'keep in touch'.

'We already have your address, telephone number and email address!' Olivier said to Mrs Caldicot. 'We will be in touch soon! We must meet again most quickly. Maybe we are all coming to England!'

Mrs Caldicot was, for a moment puzzled, until she remembered that Olivier thought he had been entertaining the Faversham Food and Fashion Fellowship for Fervent Francophiles.

'Of course,' said Mrs Caldicot, who thought that all things considered it was best this way. She hoped the Faversham Food and Fashion Fellowship for Fervent Francophiles would not be too confused when they heard from their enthusiastic Parisian penpals and asked for the recipe for 'mietes de biscuit servies a partir de la poche'.

The Parisian hosts of the champagne party drizzled off into the night; some to look for taxis, some heading to the Metro and some walking back to their apartments. Unlike London, the French capital is a lived-in city. Central Paris is home for millions, and many of those who had welcomed Mrs Caldicot and her party lived within easy walking distance of the hotel.

The travellers, dragging, pulling and carrying their luggage, then made their way into the lift or up the stairs to find their rooms. Some, unaccustomed to apparently unlimited supplies of champagne, were just a trifle on the squiffy side of sobriety; all were weary after their day of travel

'I wonder where I can buy some postcards,' said Mrs Roberts, when the last of their hosts had disappeared and the majority of the residents were busy preparing for bed.

Ruth, slightly startled, looked at her. 'Postcards?'

'Just to send to a few friends,' explained Mrs Roberts. 'If I don't send them off quickly we'll be home before they arrive.'

'I've already sent mine!' said Ruth proudly. She held up her mobile telephone, pressed a couple of keys and showed Mrs Roberts the photos and messages which her friends had already received.

'Oh no, I want to send real postcards,' said Mrs Roberts with a slight shudder of disapproval. 'You can't put those things on your mantelpiece or stick them onto your fridge.'

'The important thing is not to write: 'Wish you were here!' said Mrs Caldicot. 'I did that once when I was a young girl on holiday in Torquay with a couple of girlfriends. 'I sent the cards with the same message to a dozen people I knew, including a boy I sort of thought I fancied a bit. Two days later he turned up with his rucksack. It was very embarrassing.'

Mrs Roberts laughed.

'Ooo, I'd have been so thrilled if that had happened to me,' said Ruth.

'No you wouldn't,' said Mrs Caldicot. 'He didn't have anywhere to stay and thought he was going to stay with me and my girlfriends. Fortunately, the landlady had a very strict 'no guests in the rooms' rule and he had to go back home the same day. We all had to club together to find the money for his rail fare.'

'It was a romantic thing to do though,' said Ruth.

'I suppose it was,' admitted Mrs Caldicot.

'Was that Mr Caldicot, the man you married before Mr Jenkins?'

'Good heavens, no!' said Mrs Caldicot. 'Mr Caldicot wouldn't have done anything like that. He wasn't an overly romantic sort of fellow.'

Ruth, who was slightly startled by what Mrs Caldicot had told her, didn't say anything.

It was funny, she thought.

When she'd started work at what she knew as Caldicot House, she had been filled with a desire to help the old people living there. She was what used to be called a big-hearted girl, generous and full of simple kindness. But she really knew very little about old people. Two of her grandparents had died some years ago and she had never seen the other two who had emigrated to America and now lived in a trailer park in Florida. She hadn't ever thought of them ever having had romantic experiences.

'I'll get some cards tomorrow,' said Mrs Roberts. 'There's bound to be a little shop somewhere close to the hotel.'

The three of them then made their way up the final flight of stairs and found their rooms, which were all on the top floor. When she had deposited her own suitcase in her room, Mrs Caldicot checked to make sure all her residents were safe, comfortable and happy.

Mr Livingstone was in his bedroom and had been sitting in the room's solitary easy chair when Mrs Caldicot knocked and said who was there. 'It's only me, Mr Livingstone!'

He called out for her to enter and stood up when she entered. He had clearly been crying. Indeed, there were still tears on his cheeks. He brushed them away with the back of his hand.

'What on earth's the matter?' asked Mrs Caldicot.

Mr Livingstone took out a large handkerchief and blew his nose. 'I've been here before, you know,' he said eventually. 'Not here, not to this hotel, but to Paris.'

'On holiday?' asked Mrs Caldicot.

'Not exactly,' said Mr Livingstone. 'It was in 1942.'

'Oh,' said Mrs Caldicot. She could guess what was coming next.

'You know I flew in bombers during the War?'

Mrs Caldicot nodded.

'I was the bomb aimer. It was my job to make sure that our bombs hit the designated target.'

Mrs Caldicot nodded again. She wasn't really quite sure what to say.

'We were shot down over France and I was captured and taken to a prisoner of war camp. We were coming back from a raid. We'd dropped our bombs. It was quite successful, I think. But we got picked up by a searchlight and shot down with ack ack fire.'

Mrs Caldicot couldn't help thinking how extraordinary it was that she had known this man for some time and did not know this about him. She wondered how much else there was that she didn't know about her friends. When people have lived for 70 or 80 years or more they are bound to have experienced many things with their lives.

'How did you come to be in Paris?'

'I escaped from the prisoner of war camp I was in. A few of us got out through a tunnel which we dug. I was with an American airman. He spoke more French than I did. He was very good at it, actually. Spoke it like a native. Nice bloke. He had been about to start studying dentistry when the War had started but he'd joined up. I don't think he had to join up at all. I'm not sure America was in the War at the time and he could have gone to college. But his mother was French and he wanted to fight, as much for France as anything else I think. Through sheer luck we met up with a girl from the French Resistance and she helped us. They had this complicated route for getting Allied airmen out of France. It seems strange, since the place was awash with Germans, but one of their routes out of France involved travelling into Paris.'

'How long were you here, in the city?'

'Oh, only a couple of days. The Resistance kept us tucked away in a top floor flat in the 15th arrondissement. But we could just see the Eiffel Tower from the skylight.'

'And you've never been back here since then?'

'No,' said Mr Livingstone. 'No, this is my first time since the War.'

'What happened to your companion, the American who was going to study dentistry? Is he still alive? Are you still in touch?'

'He and the girl both died,' said Mr Livingstone. He swallowed and didn't speak for a moment. 'They were killed by the Germans. The girl and a bloke she worked with moved us in the middle of the night and we ran into a patrol. We were in a stolen Post Office van which got stopped at a checkpoint. We all ran and they both got shot. The Germans didn't have to shoot them. We weren't armed. My mate put up his hands to show he didn't have a weapon but they just shot him down. I don't think they even knew he was an escaped prisoner of war. They just shot him down because they had guns and he didn't. They shot the girl as well. She can't have been more than 15 or 16-years-old. She was a tiny little slip of a thing; not old enough to be someone's wife or girlfriend, just someone's brave daughter. I was lucky. The Frenchman and I managed to get away. He knew a way into the sewers and we spent eight hours down there before coming up miles away. And we didn't come up smelling of roses, either. Four days later I was back in England. And a week after that I was back in a bomber over Germany. I could have had some leave because I was entitled to it but I wanted to get back into the air.' He paused. There was enormous sadness in his eyes. 'I have always done any job I've had to the very best of my ability,' he said. 'But on the sorties I flew after I had escaped from the Germans, after that awful thing that happened in Paris, I made extra, special care to make sure that our bombs did the maximum amount of damage.' He took out his large handkerchief again and blew his nose. 'I know they're not all to blame but I don't think I'll ever be able to ever stop hating Germans.'

Mrs Caldicot couldn't think of anything at all worth saying. She reached out and put her arms around Mr Livingstone and hugged him. She could feel his body convulsing with the sobs and she could feel the tears falling onto her neck.

'I'll be OK in a while,' said Mr Livingstone, after a while. 'Seeing the Eiffel Tower brought everything back to me in a rush. A lot of people died in that War. They were very brave. And what the hell was it all about? Borders? Greed? Power? Saving Poland? Stopping a stupid Austrian fellow with a funny salute? Does anyone care now? Does anyone remember what it was all about?'

The two of them stayed silent for a while.

'Don't say anything to the others,' said Mr Livingstone after a while. 'I don't usually like talking about any of it. There isn't any point in dredging it all up, is there?'

Mrs Caldicot took his head in her hands and kissed him on the forehead, as you might kiss a child you didn't know terribly well but wanted very much to comfort.

'You must think I'm a big softy,' said Mr Livingstone, with a sheepish grin. He wiped his sleeve across his face, smudging the tears away.

'I think you're a very brave man; a hero,' said Mrs Caldicot with simple honesty.

After she left his room she stood in the hallway for a few moments before knocking on the next door.

For a moment she remembered the way the customs people had dealt with Mr Livingstone and the others. She knew the customs people had to do a job but did they have to be so disrespectful? And would they be quite so disrespectful if a group of middle aged, fat cat bankers in pinstripe suits had been going through customs with their Louis Vuitton luggage? She suspected that they would not have dared be quite so rude and dismissive and that thought made her even angrier. How odd, she thought, that public servants should bend their knees before rogues, crooks and tricksters but sneer at honest, hard-working people.

She shook her head, took a deep breath and knocked on the next door.

'They were lovely people,' said Mrs Peterborough who was trying to decide which of the seven nightdresses she had brought with her she should wear. She was talking about their hosts at the soiree they had attended. 'Do you think they liked my little poem?'

'I'm sure they loved it,' said Mrs Caldicot.

Mrs Peterborough blushed with delight.

'It's not how old you are that matters, but how you are old,' thought Mrs Caldicot, smiling to herself.

She had known many women in their 40s who thought and lived in the way we tend to think 80-year-olds should think and live but the always delightful corollary is that there are some people in their 80s who are well preserved in body, mind and spirit and who think and live like 40-year-olds.

'Or younger!' said Mrs Caldicot out loud.

'I beg your pardon, dear?' said Mrs Peterborough.

'Nothing,' said Mrs Caldicot, reaching out and giving Mrs Peterborough a hug.

She remembered how Mrs Peterborough had been when they had met. She had been ignored and dismissed. She might as well have been one of those red, plastic armchairs with which Mr Hawksmoor filled the lounge at the Twilight Years Rest Home. There was, she remembered, one row of chairs against one wall and another row of chairs against the opposite wall. When the residents weren't asleep, drugged with tranquillisers they didn't need, they simply sat and stared at one another. There wasn't anything much else for them to do. And even if there had been anything else to do they wouldn't have had the energy to do it.

Unlimited kindness, unconditional respect and a loving, caring environment had done wonders for Mrs Peterborough. Taking her off those damned tranquillisers had helped too.

Chapter Twelve

Britons and Americans who visit France for the first time are sometimes disappointed by the sort of breakfast usually served up at the sort of hotels which specialise in providing accommodation for tourists who aren't travelling on expense accounts, or whose costs aren't being met by a government, a government agency, a rich voluntary body or one of those international charities which always have plenty of money to spend on their executive staff but never seem to have very much to spend on the good cause which the charity claims to espouse.

When you are accustomed to starting the day with eggs, bacon, fried tomatoes, mushrooms and lashings of hot toast, and then washing the lot down with a glass of orange juice and several cups of tea, it can be disappointing to have to make do with a flaky brioche or a chunk of buttered baguette (served with a miniature pot of jam) and a rapidly cooling over-wide cup of fairly wishy washy looking café au lait.

If you like to start your morning with pancakes, hash browns, waffles, steak, sausage, ham, fries, an omelette and an unlimited supply of hot chocolate, tomato juice, milk or coffee then finding yourself expected to start the day with no more fuel than might be provided by a single, forlorn croissant can be disheartening.

But Mrs Caldicot's travelling circus (as Ruth had affectionately referred to their merry band in a late night text to Denise) was not caught out by the French preference for speed and convenience as far as breakfast is concerned, for they had come forearmed and well prepared. Mr Hewitt had brought with him a good supply of bacon, a dozen eggs, a thick sliced loaf of bread and two large boxes of cornflakes.

And so, after some rather heated discussions with the hotel's breakfast chef, who was initially reluctant to allow his cooker to be used by hotel residents, those among the party who wanted a proper breakfast enjoyed a marvellous English fry up: crispy bacon, fried eggs and proper English toast.

The chef, whose professional integrity had been soothed with a rather generous one-time donation which had made Mr Williams's wallet considerably thinner and less of a burden, had turned a blind eye. And although he had been seen to shudder, he had done his best to ignore the aroma and sizzle of bacon a-frying and eggs a-spluttering over a suitably turned up gas flame.

The Merivales, Maurice and Maple, Mr Twist, Mr Williams, Mr Roxdale, Mr Hewitt and Mr Livingstone all enjoyed a solid, full English breakfast. Mrs Peterborough, Mrs Torridge and Miss Nightingale enjoyed a magnificent, if rather unusual, breakfast comprising lashings of mulligatawny soup, copious quantities of pilchards and the remains of the tinned apricots. Ruth, Mrs Roberts and Mrs Caldicot enjoyed eggs and bacon with a side order of tinned apricots. Everyone also had a croissant and a cup of hotel coffee.

'They say you can get hardened arteries if you eat too much of this stuff,' said Mr Roxdale, enjoying another rasher of crispy bacon.

'I don't want sloppy, flippy floppy arteries,' said Mr Hewitt. 'Soggy arteries are for girls. A real man should have good, solid, hard arteries!' He looked at Mrs Merivale's plate whereupon lay a solitary rasher of bacon. 'Are you not eating that?'

Mrs Merivale shook her head. 'I'm absolutely full to the brim!'

Mr Hewitt reached across, forked the bacon and transferred it to his own plate.

Mrs Caldicot looked across at them and couldn't help smiling. Mr Roxdale was in his 80s and Mr Hewitt well into his 90s. It seemed a little late to start offering them dietary advice.

'So, where do you want to go first?' asked Mrs Caldicot, when everyone was properly fed and watered and ready for their first day in Paris. Teeth had been cleaned, hair had been combed and faces had been washed and, in the case of those who felt it appropriate and necessary, suitably decorated with coloured creams, powders and waxes.

There was, inevitably, some debate about this.

Mr Hewitt and Mr Livingstone thought they should find a shop where they could purchase fresh supplies of essential foodstuffs. They had, pointed out Mr Hewitt, exhausted their imported supplies of the essentials. Mrs Roberts said she would quite like to find a shop selling postcards. Mr Twist thought he might quite like to visit the Louvre. Mr Roxdale, who had crammed his fork and trowel into his jacket pocket, felt that a tour of the city's parks would enable him to best assess the quality of French gardening. Mrs Peterborough and Miss Nightingale said they thought they didn't mind where they went as long as they didn't go too far from a lavatory because Mrs Peterborough had drunk rather a lot of champagne the night before and had drunk two large cups of tea with her breakfast and Mrs Torridge agreed with them. Mr Williams said that at some point, if it was acceptable to everyone else, he would quite like to go into the Marais where there were some art galleries he would like to look at. Ruth, who had picked up a map and a tourist guide from the reception desk said she'd like to visit some of the shops on the Champs-Élysées. The Merivales, Maurice and Maple, said they would like to visit the Place du Tetre, walk along the banks of the Seine and go down into the student area of the 5th arrondissement. Mr Twist said in addition to taking a look at the Louvre, he thought he would like to take a look at the Quai d'Orfevres, the place where Maigret, the fictional French detective, had his offices.

It was agreed that they would do all of these things and that they would also visit the Eiffel Tower, Notre Dame, Sacre Coeur, Les Invalides, the Louvre and both the Luxembourg Gardens and the Tuileries Gardens.

Mrs Caldicot's only stipulation was that whatever they did they should do it together. 'I really don't like the idea of everyone wandering around Paris by themselves,' she whispered to Mrs Roberts.

As they discussed their plans they headed, as one body, towards the door of the hotel where Raphael stood, dignified and, it has to be said, rather pointless.

'Good mornings!' said the doorman very cheerily, addressing Mrs Caldicot. 'I fetch for you a taxi, old woman? You would like me to arrange a nightclub? A trip to Versailles in our air conditioned coach? A tour of the city by night?' He turned and leered at Mr Hewitt, who happened to be standing closest to him. 'A trip to one of our saucy nightclubs?'

'Not a bit of it!' said Mr Hewitt very firmly.

'We're going for a walk, thank you very much,' said Mrs Caldicot very firmly.

Privately she marvelled at how such an aggressive and arrogant man managed, at the same time, to be smarmy and rather creepy. He rather reminded her of Mr Hawsksmoor, the proprietor of the Twilight Years Rest Home. She shuddered involuntarily and turned to Mrs Roberts. 'I think one of us had better decide what we're doing or else we'll be standing here all day!'

'I think you're right,' agreed Mrs Roberts, who always preferred other people to make decisions whenever possible.

Mrs Caldicot cleared her throat and announced that she had made a decision.

She did so with such certainty that everyone, even Raphael the doorman, turned and looked in her direction.

'This morning we will walk through the Tuileries Gardens, go down to the Seine, stroll along the river bank and then walk up towards the Eiffel Tower and after that the Champs-Élysées,' she said. She paused for a moment. 'And then this afternoon we will do something else,' she added. And clutching the map which the hotel provided, Mrs Caldicot pointed to the left. 'We'll go that way!'

Everyone agreed that this was a splendid plan.

With Mrs Caldicot leading the way, the assembled company began to put her excellent plan into action.

'Toodle pip!' said Mr Roxdale to Raphael.

'What is that?' demanded the doorman.

'Toodle pip!' repeated Mr Roxdale. 'Tally ho! The game's afoot!'

'What is this tootle plipping?' asked Raphael, looking more puzzled than ever.

'It's the way the English say 'goodbye',' said Mr Roxdale.

'Goodbye is not right? They do not say 'goodbye'?'

'Oh no, not the proper English. That's just what they teach foreigners. The English say 'toodle pip' or 'tally ho' or 'the game's afoot'!'

'Tootle peep,' said Raphael, trying it out. 'Tally how!'

'Close!' said Mr Roxdale. 'Toodle pip old bean!'

'Tootle peep old bean,' repeated Raphael. 'Tally how!'

'And 'the game's afoot'! Try that. Very popular with the younger Brits.'

'The games afeet,' said Raphael.

'That'll do nicely,' said Mr Roxdale, hurrying after the rest.

'You will teach me more proper English?' Raphael called after him.

'Pleasure!' replied Mr Roxdale. 'Another lesson tonight when we get back.'

'Thank you!' cried Raphael. 'Tootle peep old bean, the games afeet!'

'What did that idiot doorman say?' asked Mr Hewitt when Mr Roxdale caught up.

'He tried to say 'toodle pip',' said Mr Roxdale. 'I'm teaching him English.'

'Splendid idea!' agreed Mr Hewitt rubbing his hands together in delight. 'Can I help?'

'Think up some more phrases we can teach him,' said Mr Roxdale. 'He's an unpleasant fellow, isn't he?'

'I've heard he thinks very highly of himself,' said Mr Hewitt. 'Indeed, I suspect he thinks of nothing else.'

The two of them laughed.

As the party arrived at the end of the street, wherein lay their hotel, they passed a pavement stall selling oysters.

'Oh look!' said Mr Williams, excitedly. 'I must have a dozen of those to start the day.' The others watched as the man behind the counter shucked a dozen oysters and put them onto a plate. 'Casanova used to eat 50 of these every morning for breakfast,' said Mr Williams who loved fish and shellfish of all kinds. He was fond of cockles and winkles, adored whitebait and would walk ten miles in bare feet and on stony ground to find himself next to a well salted, nicely smoked bloater. But oysters, so rarely available on the menu at Caldicot House, were for him the holy grail of all seafood delicacies.

'Really!' said Mrs Roberts, who sounded rather startled and not a little concerned.

'Oh don't worry!' laughed Mr Williams. 'I'm far too old for oysters to have any useful effect on me.'

Mrs Roberts did not look entirely convinced.

'Would anyone like to try one?' Mr Williams asked when he had squeezed lemon juice over his oysters.

Everyone instinctively backed away a foot or two.

‘I’d like to try one,’ said Mrs Caldicot, not entirely sure why she’d said it and surprising herself more than anyone else.

‘Chew it a couple of times and then swallow it,’ advised Mr Williams.

The rest then stared with a mixture of respect, astonishment and horror as Mrs Caldicot chewed and then swallowed her oyster. She declined the offer of a second.

‘What was it like?’ Mrs Roberts asked Mrs Caldicot.

‘Horrid,’ whispered Mrs Caldicot. ‘It was absolutely horrid; slithery, rubbery and tasteless.’ She shuddered.

She and the others watched in horror as Mr Williams continued to devour his plateful of seafood with great relish.

‘Splendid!’ he said, wiping his lips when he had finished. ‘Now I know I’m definitely in Paris!’

He handed the empty plate back to the stall holder.

They walked away from the street stall and continued their walk towards the park.

‘What was that oyster like?’ Ruth asked Mrs Caldicot.

‘It was like swallowing a bit of lemony rubber,’ answered Mrs Caldicot with a shudder. ‘I don’t know why I did that.’ She thought for a moment and then she smiled. ‘Yes, I do. Now I can tell my husband that I’ve tried oysters and I don’t like them!’

As they walked, an excited Mrs Roberts caught up with them. She was slightly out of breath. She held up a small white, paper envelope. ‘Look!’ she said delightedly. ‘I managed to buy some postcards from that little shop we passed along the way.’

They all tiptoed around a spot on the pavement where an artist had been busy using coloured chalks to decorate the pavement. He had drawn a huge tropical island. There was yellow sand, green and brown palm trees, dark blue sea and lighter blue sky. The artist was busy drawing a mermaid, sitting on the sand. The mermaid was looking into the sea rather wistfully.

‘Did you get the stamps you wanted?’ asked Mrs Caldicot.

‘I asked the man in the shop about stamps,’ said Mrs Roberts.

‘I’m very impressed,’ said Mrs Caldicot, wondering how long it would be before she could get a drink to wash away the unpleasant sensation the oyster had left in her mouth.

'Well, actually, I didn't really ask him,' admitted Mrs Roberts. 'I just pointed to the little rectangular space where you normally stick your stamp, raised an eyebrow and tried to look quizzical.'

'What did he say?'

'I don't know what he said but he just gave me my change and shook his head.'

'Don't worry! I'm sure we'll be able to find some stamps for sale,' said Mrs Caldicot.

It was a beautiful spring day and the trees of Paris, mostly plane and horse chestnut in this part of the city, were already in full leaf. They were, pointed out Mr Roxdale, a good month or so ahead of the trees in England. The party walked on, chattering happily, pointing things out to one another, laughing, enjoying the unique and special smells and sights and sounds of a city most of them had never visited before. Only Mr Williams knew Paris really well. A decade or two earlier he had had a small photographic studio in Paris. His photographs had been shown regularly in the city's galleries and had been reproduced in the expensive magazines.

Mrs Caldicot looked around at her companions and smiled. It was good to have friends. She missed Jenkins terribly but was reassured with the thought that she'd see him in a couple of days. She felt a twinge in her knee occasionally and her back was a trifle stiff. She thought that perhaps the bed in the hotel had been a little too soft. Her spine needed more support at night than it did when she had been half a century younger. Growing old can be a bit of a nuisance sometimes but, she thought to herself with a little smile, it is far better than the alternative. Her father was the first person she'd heard say that. And he'd probably got it from his father. But as she looked around at her friends, all enjoying their first morning in Paris, and the stiffness in her back seemed to ease a little. Maybe springtime in Paris had some sort of healing quality. Suddenly she felt 18. She remembered reading somewhere that although the body ages and weakens, and the mind grows older and sometimes slower too, the human spirit never ages. When we age we may have difficulty in climbing stairs or leaping over fences, and our memories may not be quite as sharp as they were at 14, but we still feel the same inside as we felt when we were young and were just setting out on the great adventure which is life.

It is a widely held myth that both the human body and the human mind must inevitably deteriorate in all respects as the years trundle by with increasing speed. The myth is perpetuated because it is convenient and it fits society's preconceived notion of how the elderly should be.

The young sometimes find it uncomfortable to accept that wrinkly and slightly wobbly old folk may be just as bright as they are and this is perhaps because they realise that when intelligence is added to wisdom gained through experience, the sum of the two is considerably more potent than the one alone.

The party waited at the traffic lights, crossed the Rue de Rivoli, and entered the Tuileries Gardens, the huge, ornamental park which lies between the Louvre Palace and the Place de la Concorde.

A small guidebook which Mrs Roberts had picked up at the hotel receptionist desk, explained that the gardens, created by Catherine de Medici, were originally the private gardens of the Palace. They were, she read and explained, first begun in the 16th century and only became a public park after the French Revolution.

'The gardens have for two centuries been a popular place for fashionable Parisians to stroll, meet and have picnics,' announced Mrs Roberts.

Miss Nightingale, as excited as a child, danced and skipped on the dusty paths, admiring the beautiful spring flowers and the neatly trimmed hedges. She and Mrs Peterborough posed together, resting each side of a grey, stone statue of a supersized and very obviously naked Adonis, while Ruth took their photograph with the camera on her mobile telephone. Miss Nightingale and Mrs Peterborough were so full of laughter that they could hardly stand up straight. Ruth, catching the giggle mood, had to take the photograph half a dozen times before she managed to get a picture that didn't cut off Mrs Peterborough's head or Miss Nightingale's feet.

While Mr Hewitt and Mr Roxdale tackled a few of the weeds that were growing in the garden's flower borders, the rest of the party stood and watched a young boy playing with a small, wooden yacht on a boating pond. They then walked on a few yards and stood for a few moments and listened to a young girl playing a violin. They marvelled at the amount of money which visitors and tourists had tossed into the girl's empty violin case.

They watched as a painfully thin jogger in his 30s leant against a tree and stretched his hamstrings and they said 'No thank you' to the invitations to buy from a North African citizen who was selling carved wooden bowls which he had carefully laid out on a large plaid rug.

'The rug makes it easy for him to make a quick getaway,' explained Mr Williams. 'If he spots a policeman coming he'll just pick up the rug by the four corners and scarper. The police never catch these fellows – they're just too fast.'

They admired several human statues.

One individual (it was impossible to tell whether the person underneath was male or female) had draped her or himself in a green robe, put a green crown on his or her head and painted his or her face green. He or she was holding a green cardboard torch.

'Look,' said Mrs Roberts. 'The statue of liberty!'

Ruth took a photograph. She must, thought Mrs Caldicot, have already taken several hundred photographs. It was a good job she wasn't using a camera that used film.

A few yards away another person (once again unidentifiable by sex) had dressed him or herself as a French King. The King was standing perfectly still and had a feathered hat at his or her feet into which passers-by had tossed some coins.

An artist, sitting on one of the green, metal chairs with which the park was well supplied, was drawing a young girl who was sitting on one of the fixed wooden and metal benches. The artist wore a grubby-looking, grey jumper and a pair of faded jeans. He seemed much older than you might expect a street artist to be; too old to be a student. Maybe, thought Mrs Caldicot, he was a serious artist, living in a tiny attic room in Montmartre and drawing tourists so that he could buy paint, canvas and food. He had a small, khaki coloured rucksack on the floor beside him. It appeared to be almost empty.

The model, the girl he was sketching, wore a camel coloured coat and had a light blue scarf wrapped round her neck. She had dark hair, worn long, and was hatless. A young man, smartly but casually dressed and presumably the girl's boyfriend, fiancé or husband was standing beside the artist, watching his every movement, as though keen to ensure that the girl's beauty was captured adequately.

The artist was sketching with charcoal on a sheet of grey paper and his hand moved swiftly and confidently. The drawing was remarkably life-like.

Mrs Caldicot wondered if the young couple were, perhaps, on their honeymoon. The finished drawing would, in any case, doubtless be greatly appreciated and treasured. Maybe it would be framed when they got home. Maybe it would remain rolled, with an increasingly fragile rubber band, holding it furled; destined to lie in a box in the attic. She found herself hoping, and even believing, that it would end up very nicely framed and hanging in the hall. Visitors would admire it and the couple would explain how they had it done in the Tuileries Gardens in Paris by a nice chap called Pierre or Marcel or Stephan who wanted 20 euros but agreed to 15 euros. They would, perhaps, always wonder if Pierre or Marcel or Stephan ever became famous. They might wonder if their charcoal sketch could be worth millions.

A couple were playing chess. The two players were each seated on metal chairs. The board and pieces were on a third chair, between them. The woman, a redhead, was slightly built. The other player, a man, much older, was huge and must have weighed twice as much. Judging from the state of the board, the older man appeared to be winning.

Mrs Peterborough was driven to rhyme.

'A red headed woman called Kate
Played chess with a bloke twice her weight
The bloke took her queen
With a move she'd not seen
And shocked her by calling out 'Mate!'

The players were concentrating hard and they did not look up. Maybe they did not speak English, thought Mrs Caldicot. Maybe they did not realise that the limerick was about them. Maybe they didn't like limericks. Mr Livingstone did, very much, and he once again led the applause.

A little further on an even older artist, this one seemingly in his sixties, white haired, white bearded, was sitting on a metal chair and bent over a small easel and was concentrating hard on a watercolour painting. Mrs Caldicot would have expected him to be doing a sketch from memory of the Eiffel Tower or maybe the green bouquiniste book stalls along the edge of the river Seine. But he wasn't. He was drawing a French pastoral scene. Fields, trees, meadows, flowers, a small river and half a dozen cows. Mrs Caldicot wondered if the picture was taken from memory or just taken from the man's imagination. It was exquisitely worked. Several finished paintings were arranged on a couple of adjacent chairs. They were very reasonably priced.

'What a beautiful painting!' whispered Mrs Caldicot to Mr Williams, who was standing beside her. Mr Williams, who did not speak, merely nodded his agreement.

'I can't help wondering why this poor chap is having to sell his paintings in a park,' said Mrs Caldicot. 'And they are so reasonably priced.' She wondered whether or not to purchase one but then remembered that she had brought very little money with her. The group had brought their cash with them as communal funds, looked after by Mr Twist. Apart from a few euros for incidentals, she had no money of her own in her handbag.

'I've certainly seen stuff in art galleries that wasn't as good,' agreed Mr Williams.

'So, why is this poor fellow having to sit out here and sell his work this way? Why won't an art gallery put his paintings on display? Surely they could market them for him?'

'Art is like music and writing,' explained Mr Williams. 'It's not just about talent. It's also about how well you can sell yourself and present your work. It's about who you meet and, more than anything else, it's about luck. Success is merely a combination of talent and luck. You need both and of the two I would say that luck is the most important. When I first came to Paris I happened to meet a fellow who was starting a new photographic gallery. It was empty and had only just been decorated. I walked past his new and empty shop and saw him struggling to move a desk he'd had delivered. I called in and helped him put the desk where he wanted it. As a thank you he took me into a bar and bought me a beer. When we talked I mentioned that I was trying to make my way as a photographer. He asked to see some of my pictures. I happened to have some in my bag. I'd just collected them from the developer. The fellow had empty walls and no clients. He was delighted to pay for some of my photographs to be enlarged and framed and hung on his walls. And because a few of them sold he continued to hang my pictures. Then other gallery owners saw that this chap was making money out of me and I was on my way.'

'But it was talent that made you successful,' said Mrs Caldicot.

'A little bit, perhaps,' said Mr Williams, modestly. 'But it was more the result of that meeting with the gallery owner. I was lucky that he was trying to move that desk by himself. I was lucky that I wasn't in a hurry and I could go in and help him. I was lucky that he had a new gallery with empty walls. I was lucky that I happened to have some of my photographs with me. People say that they make your own luck but that has never been my experience. I didn't make any of my luck.' He shrugged. 'If I'd gone into that gallery three months later with a portfolio of photographs, the gallery owner would have probably sent me away. His walls were by then fully covered with photographs for sale.'

'But you stopped to help that man in his shop,' said Mrs Caldicot. 'That was a kind gesture. You deserved the luck.'

'Maybe,' agreed Mr Williams. 'But I knew another chap at that time, he too was trying to make it as a photographer. He took brilliant pictures. He had an eye and an amazing talent. He would walk the streets of Paris at night taking pictures of people coming out of nightclubs and of prostitutes on the pavements. He was a master of taking pictures in the rain, with lights reflected in the puddles. Everything he took was in black and white. He never took anything in colour. But because he didn't have any money he slept on a couch in a friend's tiny one room cellar near the river. It was damp and everything he wore smelt of mould. He never bathed and he stank. Whenever he went into a gallery to try to persuade them to look at his pictures, they threw him out. He never did make it. He had loads of talent but no luck.'

'What happened to him?' asked Mrs Caldicot.

'Eventually, someone persuaded him to take snaps of the tourists to earn a little money. He sold his cameras and bought one of those Polaroid instant cameras. He stood outside a café on the Place de l'Opera and took pictures of British and American tourists. He scratched a living doing that. When he started, he swore he was doing it just to get onto his feet. He found a small studio apartment of his own. He got into a relationship with a prostitute who worked the same stretch of pavement. They lived together but then she fell ill and he had to keep them both. Twenty years after he'd started with his Polaroid camera, he was still doing the same thing: snaps of the tourists sitting enjoying their coffees and their pastries. When I became a bit successful and had a little money I offered to lend him money so that he could buy a proper camera and start taking decent pictures again. But he wouldn't take the money. I told him the money was a gift, and that I didn't want it repaying, but he refused.'

'Is he still there, still taking pictures of tourists?'

'Oh no. He died some years ago. His girlfriend, the prostitute had tuberculosis – probably caught from a client. He caught it off her. They both died of it. It was like something out of a tragic opera. Ironic, really, that he spent his best years taking Polaroid snaps outside the Opera building.'

They had walked no more than a third of a mile from the hotel, walking through the Tuileries Gardens on their way to the Seine, enjoying some glorious Easter sunshine on their first day in the French capital, when Mr Livingstone spotted a small crowd of people a little way ahead. He hurried on, calling for the others to join him. Mr Roxdale and Mr Hewitt did so with some reluctance for they had just spotted a number of overly enthusiastic weeds growing in a bed of beautifully coloured cyclamen plants. The two keen gardeners were having a whale of a time tidying up Paris's premier gardens.

'By golly, we can show these Frenchies a thing or two about weeding!' said Mr Hewitt, wielding the trowel which he had brought with him.

'There's nothing to touch good old-fashioned British weeding,' agreed Mr Roxdale, who was working with his fork. 'The Frogs don't have the patience for it.'

'Nor the talent,' said Mr Hewitt. 'There's a talent required for good weeding.'

Mr Roxdale nodded enthusiastically as he removed another dandelion, this one with a tap root a good nine inches long. 'You're absolutely right about that, Mr Hewitt.'

The crowd which Mr Livingstone had spotted consisted largely of tourists.

The people had gathered around two men who were using a large cardboard box as an impromptu table and who were inviting people in the crowd to make bets on the position of the Queen of Hearts card.

The man handling the cards was wearing an open-necked sports shirt and knee length white tailored shorts. The shorts had a sharp crease down the front of each leg. He was also wearing knee-length, white socks and tennis shoes. It is nigh on impossible to look dignified while wearing shorts but it is certainly impossible to look threatening or dangerous. How can anyone take a card sharp seriously when he is wearing white shorts with a crease down the legs? That, presumably, was the idea.

The man was moving the Queen of Hearts around on his makeshift table with two other cards, one of which was the six of clubs and the other was the nine of spades. It was, Mrs Caldicot realised quickly, the old 'Three Card Monte' or 'Find the Lady' game which is always popular with street tricksters. The man handling the cards seemed surprisingly slow and when he stopped, after moving the cards around, it wasn't particularly difficult to see which of the three cards was the Queen of Hearts.

Mr Livingstone, followed by the others, joined the crowd and looked on as first one and then another spectator bet money on the position of the picture card. The card sharp had put a crease into each of the three cards and he moved them about on the cardboard box with practiced ease.

Each of the first three spectators won and pocketed their winnings with clear delight, waving the money they had won in the air with tremendous glee.

'Those are hundred euro notes!' said Mr Twist who, as a former income tax inspector, had a great deal of respect for notes of any denomination but more particularly, perhaps, for notes of a large denomination.

'Lots of people seem to be winning,' said Mr Roxdale.

'Perhaps the man handling the cards isn't very good,' said Mr Livingstone.

'That woman just won at least five hundred euros!' said Mrs Roberts, in awe.

'The winners are all colleagues of the tricksters,' whispered Mr Williams. 'They're stooges.'

'Surely they can't be,' said Mrs Caldicot. 'The woman who won the money looks very respectable.'

And it was quite true that the stooges did not look in the slightest bit disreputable.

The woman who had won, spent some time ostentatiously depositing her winnings in a large blue handbag with a solid looking brass clasp. It was the sort of handbag that Mrs Margaret Thatcher, the Iron Lady, would have been proud to carry on her arm. The winner, the owner of the handbag, was wearing a blue-grey tweed skirt with a matching jacket and a white blouse. She wore a rather nifty, old-fashioned little hat with some fruit and feathers on it, and a pair of white gloves. She had a double string of pearls around her neck and wore large, pearl earrings. The pearls were all far too large to be real but they gave her a convincing look of stability and solidity. You don't expect a woman wearing a tweed twin set and pearls to be a gangster's moll.

'She's a stooge,' insisted Mr Williams, who was not taken in. 'She's part of the trickster's team.' He leant closer and smiled at Mrs Caldicot. 'Not all villains have curling moustachios and darting eyes.'

'No, I suppose they don't!' agreed Mrs Caldicot. 'They wouldn't be very good at it if they did, would they?'

'Exactly!'

'What about that man over there,' said Mrs Caldicot, nodding towards a young man in a crumpled, white linen suit and a dented Panama hat. 'He just won quite a lot of money. Surely he can't be part of the team too!'

'Oh he is,' said Mr Williams. 'The confidence tricksters have quite a big team these days. He's one of the stooges. And so too is the man dressed like a bookie from the 1970s and the chap on his right who is dressed like a TV weatherman.'

'The fellow in the blue jumper with clouds on it?'

'That's the one.'

As he spoke, a young man in jeans and a red shirt, who was clearly travelling with his girlfriend, took out his wallet, removed all the money and confidently held it out towards the man handling the cards.

'You can tell the stooges because they all have a meanness and a ruthlessness about them. And somehow although they try to dress the part, they never quite get everything just right. The chap who looks like a bookie is wearing a three piece checked suit but if you look down you'll see he has scruffy trainers on his feet. No ordinary person wearing that suit would have shoes like that. The woman who is masquerading as an English lady is over the top and about 30 years out-of-date. She probably based her outfit on a picture she saw in an old magazine and then picked up the clothes at one of the Paris flea markets. And would a woman dressed like that really be prepared to bet so much on the turn of a card? Look at her gloves, too. The fingertips are black. They haven't been washed for ages.'

'What about that one?' asked Mrs Caldicot, who was fascinated by everything she was hearing. She indicated the young man in the jeans and red shirt.

'He's a real punter and he's about to lose his holiday money,' said Mr Williams, rather sadly. 'He had a long chat with his girlfriend before getting out his money.'

'How do you know so much about these people?' asked Mrs Caldicot.

'I lived in Paris for a while when I was taking photographs. A fellow I shared a flat with for a while lost all his money to one of these tricksters. There are quite a few of these gangs working the tourist spots in Paris.'

Sure enough, less than a minute later the young man and his girlfriend were walking away from the card sharp looking shaken and, it has to be said, rather frightened. The girl was in tears. The card handler had put the winnings into the back pocket of his jeans. Mrs Caldicot felt desperately sorry for the young couple; their holiday clearly ruined. She knew that the young man had risked their money through greed and that logically he was to blame for their loss but she nevertheless found herself wondering about the card sharp and his cronies who were so cold-bloodedly parting tourists from their money.

'I can see where the card is,' announced Mr Twist with great confidence. 'I spotted it every time.'

'Don't even think about it,' Mr Williams warned him.

'I can win a lot of money at this game,' insisted Mr Twist. He sounded confident and determined. 'I've noticed that there's a small crease in the corner of the Queen card.'

The problem with Mr Twist was that he was a bit like an old dog who has spent his whole life obediently doing what he was told to do; he was, if you like, accustomed to his collar and lead. As a tax inspector he had been restricted by rules and regulations. And when his life had fallen apart and he had ended up living rough on a traffic island, he had been bullied by just about everyone with whom he had come into contact.

But now, released from decades of confinement, he was not at all sure what to do and, more importantly, what not to do.

Should he walk away, putting temptation behind him?

Or should be accept the challenge, take what seemed to be a non-existent risk and enrich his newly found friends by winning a big chunk of money.

The trouble was that Mr Twist was desperately keen to impress his friends. And the need to impress is a potent and dangerous driving force which has led many people to make many errors and which has produced not a few embarrassments.

The woman with the large handbag bet again. And again she won several hundred euros.

'She won six hundred euros that time!' said Mr Twist.

'That crease has been put there on purpose to make you think that you can beat him,' said Mr Williams. 'But you can't beat these guys. They're professionals and they're very good at what they do. The guy who is manipulating the cards could probably deal off the top, off the bottom and out of the middle. He could probably make those cards stand on end and sing La Marseillaise if he wanted them to.'

'Come on,' said Mrs Caldicot firmly. 'We ought to be moving on.'

She rounded up her party and began to lead them away, heading once more towards the river Seine.

'Amazing,' said Mr Livingstone. 'I think I'll get myself a cardboard box and three cards, learn that trick and try it in our High Street on a Saturday afternoon. It can't be that difficult.'

'Learn to run fast and far before you try that,' said Mr Roxdale who was not driven to such flights of fancy. 'If the police spot you they'll chase you for miles. And if the police don't get you then one of the people you've bilked will probably follow you home shouting rude things and hitting you with a handbag or an umbrella.'

'Ah,' said Mr Livingstone who had gout in the large toe of his left foot, a right knee permanently crippled with rheumatoid arthritis and more than a touch of osteoarthritis in his left hip sighed rather sadly as another wild dream hit the dust. 'I don't think I'd be too good at the running bit,' he said. 'Or the 'dodging the handbag' bit.'

They wandered off together, still marvelling at the size of the crowd which had gathered around the man with the cardboard box and the playing cards.

There were, Mrs Caldicot, estimated over 30 people in the crowd.

'Look over there,' said Mr Williams quietly. He pointed to a short, tubby, scruffy man in jeans and a leather jacket who was standing holding a bicycle. 'That's one of the look-out men.'

Mrs Caldicot peered at him, puzzled. 'What do you mean 'look-out' men?'

'There will be two or three of them spread around,' said Mr Williams. 'They call them 'watchers'. If one of them sees a policeman approaching, he'll shout and ride the bicycle over to the man manipulating the cards. The card manipulator will climb on the bicycle and pedal off to a prearranged meeting place. It doesn't matter if the accomplices get caught. What could anyone charge them with? But the card manipulator could be identified. And, besides, he's important because he's the one with the dexterity and the skill to move the cards around and con the tourists.'

'So how many people are involved in the gang?' asked Mrs Caldicot, astonished.

'Probably about a dozen altogether. I once followed them and watched them all meet for the payout. The stooges who appear to have won money hand it all back to the boss and then everyone is paid their wages.'

'How can they possibly make enough money to pay so many people?'

'Easily! They'll probably bilk seven or eight tourists of their money in less than half an hour. And they don't play for euros. They play for hundreds of euros. So they can easily make 2,000 euros in half an hour. That's plenty to provide a pay-out for everyone and leave a lot of money left for the card sharp and the boss who organises the whole thing and recruits the members of the gang. And don't forget there is no rent to pay, and there are no overheads and no taxes! When they've shared out the spoils they split up, meet somewhere else half an hour or so later and then repeat the whole thing. In an average sort of day they'll bilk tourists of between 10,000 and 20,000 euros. The stooges and look-out men will each get 100 to 150 euros a day, and the card sharp and the boss will share the big money.'

'Crumbs!' said Mrs Caldicot. 'I hadn't realised it was such a big operation.'

'In a fairly average month, one of these gangs can take half a million euros off tourists. That's why the police take them seriously. That money would have probably been spent on coffees and cakes and souvenirs, and once the crooks have the money a good deal of it goes abroad and is lost to the economy. Plus there's the fact that the victims may have lost most or even all of their holiday spending money. Some of them will be too embarrassed to say anything to anyone but quite a few will tell their friends and their relatives what happened and then the city of Paris gets a bad name and people don't want to come here on their holidays because they're frightened they'll be conned out of their money too.'

'How long did you live in Paris?'

'Several years! I was lucky with my life. We all have a mountain we want to climb and I realised early on that my particular mountain wasn't out of my reach. My desire was simply to earn my living taking photographs – no more and no less. The thing is that I worked out quite early on in life that satisfaction comes not from work in itself, or from play, but from competition and from overcoming hurdles, even if those hurdles are ones which we ourselves have created. That might not be true for everyone but it was the case for me. In the end, we can all only climb to the top of the mountain we have chosen to climb. Therein, perhaps, lies the answer to happiness for if we choose a mountain which is too grand for our talents, our perseverance and, most important of all, our supply of luck, then we must be doomed to disappointment.'

'And you were obviously very successful at your chosen profession,' said Mrs Caldicot.

Mr Williams looked at her.

'Judging by the money people pay for your photographs,' said Mrs Caldicot, looking round to make sure that none of the others heard her. She knew that Mr Williams, an exceptionally modest man, did not want the others to know that his pictures sold for many thousands of pounds. His modesty was genuine and simple, and not a result of any desire to hide the fact of his wealth from his friends.

'Oh, I was very lucky,' said Mr Williams with a big smile. 'I was in Paris at the right time and I met a gallery owner who liked my pictures. There was a fashion for black and white street photographs at the time; pictures of ordinary people doing ordinary things; pictures of bread shops and cafes and the girls hanging around in the streets looking for customers. If that gallery owner hadn't taken my pictures I could have ended up photographing weddings or taking pictures for an advertising agency. It was all luck, really. There were probably better photographers out there taking pictures for postcard publishers.'

'But you made your luck,' said Mrs Caldicot. 'You came to Paris. And you helped that gallery owner when he was just starting out.'

'No, I was just fortunate,' insisted Mr Williams. 'I came to Paris because in the 1950s it was cheaper here than in London. And my girlfriend was coming here to work as a dancer. I didn't come here with the clear intention of becoming successful. I did no market research. Unbeknownst to me, I wanted to take the sort of pictures that people wanted at the time.' He laughed. 'How's that for dumb luck?'

They had by now crossed the Tuileries Gardens and from where they were standing they could look across the Place de La Concorde, right up the Champs-Élysées and see the Arc de Triomphe in the distance. They could now also see the Eiffel Tower, glimmering and sparkling in the spring sunshine.

'Can we go to that big tower?' asked Miss Nightingale, excitedly. She clapped her hands together in excitement.

'I expect there will be a shop there selling stamps for my postcards,' said Mrs Roberts, confidently.

'It looks rather a long way away,' said Mrs Torridge, rather doubtfully. 'I'm running a bit short of petrol and I'm honestly not sure my legs are going to get me that far.' She had brought Mr Torridge with her in a shopping bag. When Mrs Caldicot had suggested that she leave his ashes in the hotel bedroom, Mrs Torridge had explained that she'd thought of that but had decided that Mr Torridge had never seen Paris and that she thought it would be unfair to bring him this far and then leave him in the hotel.

'We could take a taxi,' suggested Mr Livingstone.

'We wouldn't all fit into a taxi,' Mrs Caldicot pointed out. 'We'd need three taxis. And where are we going to find three taxis all free at the same time?'

'We could catch a boat,' suggested Mr Williams.

They all looked at him as if he'd said something silly.

'There's a sort of bus service on the river Seine,' explained Mr Williams. 'It's called the Batobus. There are stops along the river bank where passengers can get on and off. There's a stop not far from here. We can catch the boat and ride all the way up to the Eiffel Tower. Then we can get off the boat, as fresh as daisies, and go up the Eiffel Tower in the lift.'

'Oo, I think I might get seasick,' said Ruth looking rather worried. 'I've never been on a ship before.'

'It isn't a ship, it's only a river boat,' said Mr Williams kindly. 'And you mustn't worry about being sick because the river is as smooth as a pond.'

'Oh,' said Ruth. 'Oh, that's all right then.' She sounded relieved.

It was generally agreed that catching the river bus was a splendid idea and so they made their way to a pedestrian crossing which would take them to the river bank and the nearby boat stop.

It was while they were waiting to cross the road that Mrs Caldicot realised that Mr Twist was missing.

Panicking somewhat, she looked around for him. 'Has anyone seen Mr Twist?' she said. She said it again; a bit louder.

'I was chatting to him a few minutes ago,' said Mr Livingstone. 'He can't have gone far.'

'He was with us when we were watching those men with the cards,' said Mrs Torridge. 'He said he could see which card was the Queen of Hearts. He said the man with the cards wasn't all that good at moving the cards about.'

'I haven't seen him for a while,' said Mr Roxdale. 'Do you think he could have been kidnapped? I've heard there's a lot of that goes on in big cities.'

'Why would anyone kidnap Mr Twist?' asked Mr Livingstone. 'He's a very nice chap, but he hasn't got any money!'

'He's got all our money,' said Mrs Caldicot. 'He's good with money so I gave him all our euros to look after. He's got the rest of our lottery winnings – everything except whatever personal spending money we all brought with us. He understands all about exchange rates and he had a money belt underneath his shirt.'

'But no one would know that,' Mrs Roberts pointed out. 'He's not going to walk around waving his money belt around.'

'No, I suppose not,' agreed Mrs Caldicot. She sighed as a hundred awful scenarios flashed through her mind. 'Oh dear, it's all my fault. I should have looked after everyone better. Maybe he's got lost? What if he's fallen down and hurt himself? What if he has suddenly been taken ill? What if he got mugged? People get mugged all the time in cities. Maybe someone just wanted to steal his watch and they hit him on the head.'

'I heard of someone being robbed for their shoes,' said Mrs Peterborough. 'He had a pair of those fancy pumps that are so fashionable with young people. They have little lights in the heels which light up when you walk.'

'Mr Twist's shoes didn't light up when he walked,' said Mr Roxdale with certainty. 'They were just rather old, ordinary brown shoes. They were a bit worn down at the heel to be honest with you. I noticed that. And the sole of one shoe was coming a bit loose. I saw it flapping about a bit.'

'Which shoe was that?' asked Mr Livingstone.

Mr Roxdale thought for a moment. 'I think it was the left,' he said at last.

'What difference does it make which shoe it was that had a loose sole?' asked Mrs Roberts, who never really got cross but was perhaps a little sharper than she would have been if she hadn't been quite so worried.

'I didn't say it made a difference,' said Mr Roxdale. 'But Mr Livingstone asked me.'

'At a time like this the police always say that every bit of information you have is important,' said Mr Livingstone rather defensively. 'Anyway, I don't see how he could have got lost,' he continued. 'We're a pretty noticeable bunch. A bunch of OAPs wandering around a park in the middle of Paris. And we've been in the park for ages.'

'We'll have to retrace our steps and look for him,' said Mrs Caldicot quite firmly, taking charge and making a decision.

And so they turned round and started to walk back the way they had come.

'Don't you think we'd better spread out?' asked Mrs Roberts.

Mrs Caldicot agreed that this was a very good idea and repeated the suggestion. The band of searchers therefore spread out into a long line.

'Keep an eye on the person either side of you,' Mrs Caldicot instructed everyone. 'We don't want to lose anyone else.'

‘I haven’t got anyone to the right of me,’ pointed out Mr Roxdale, who was on the right flank.

Mrs Caldicot asked Mrs Roberts to go on the right edge of the line and asked Ruth to go on the far left of the line.

And they started searching for Mr Twist.

Chapter Thirteen

They found Mr Twist just under fifteen minutes later.

He was sitting on a green park bench by himself.

He had his hands over his face and his sobs could be heard some distance away.

He looked, thought Mrs Caldicot, like King Lear bemoaning his fate. She wondered what on earth had happened to upset him so much.

'Wait here please,' said Mrs Caldicot to the others, and she rushed ahead to find out what was wrong.

It took her several minutes to calm Mr Twist down enough so that he could tell her what had happened.

'I've lost all our money,' he admitted at last, between sobs.

He explained that he had been so convinced that he could spot the position of the Queen of Hearts that he had taken the group's money out of his money belt and had within moments lost the whole lot on the turn of a couple of cards.

'I thought if I won more money everyone would be so pleased with me,' he said. 'I thought we could have really posh meals in smart restaurants.'

Disappointed though she was, Mrs Caldicot could not for one moment bring herself to be cross with Mr Twist.

She sat down on the bench beside him and put an arm around him.

For a woman who was in charge of a group of old aged pensioners now stuck in a foreign country with no money, she felt surprisingly calm and relaxed. Their hotel was paid for. They had their return tickets for the Eurostar train. And the hotel would serve them breakfast every morning.

It is no secret, she thought to herself, that we are not masters of our own fate. We may like to think that although we may not be able to control our destiny, we may be able to nudge it occasionally in the direction we would find most congenial, but the reality is that the big decisions in life are taken for us by fate.

And fate is sometimes rather more whimsical than we might like it to be.

'I didn't lose it all at once,' he said, as though this made it more acceptable. 'I lost half of it and then I thought I could win back what I'd lost with the rest of it.'

'It doesn't matter,' said Mrs Caldicot.

'I thought you'd like me more if I won a lot of money for us,' said Mr Twist.

'We couldn't like you any more than we do,' said Mrs Caldicot. 'And we don't need lots of money to have a good time.'

'You've been so good to me,' said Mr Twist, tears rolling down his cheeks.

'We love having you with us,' said Mrs Caldicot. 'And we couldn't like you any more than we do!' she said again.

Mr Twist responded with more sobs.

'I'll tell the others you were robbed,' said Mrs Caldicot, who realised that in addition to feeling guilty at having lost their nest-egg, Mr Twist was desperately ashamed that he had gambled away their money and lost.

'No, no,' said Mr Twist with a shake of his head. 'No, you mustn't do that.' He took out a large, red handkerchief and blew his nose rather noisily. Mr Caldicot thought that it sounded rather like a mating elephant she'd once heard on a television wildlife programme. 'I don't want you to lie for me. I have to tell them the truth.' He paused and blew his nose again. 'They're my friends.'

And so Mr Twist told the rest of the party the truth, and although they were quite shocked and certainly rather disappointed that now they wouldn't be able to go on the boat on the river Seine or up the Eiffel Tower or into the Louvre to see the Mona Lisa, because they didn't have enough money to pay for the tickets they would need for those things, no one blamed Mr Twist, although he said they should because, after all, it had been entirely his fault that they no longer had any money.

And slowly it dawned on everyone that in addition to not having any money to go on the Batobus boat on the River Seine, or to buy tickets for the lift up the Eiffel tower, they didn't have any money to buy meals.

‘I’ve still got nearly a quarter of a pocket full of biscuit crumbs!’ said Miss Nightingale cheerfully. ‘We can all share those.’

‘And there is a tin of Miss Nightingale’s mulligatawny soup left over at the hotel,’ said Mrs Peterborough.

‘I’ve got half a packet of peppermints,’ said Mr Roxdale.

And in a rather strange way, although it didn’t offer much of a realistic solution to their problem, all this information cheered them all up somewhat because it reminded them that whatever happened they were not alone and never would be because they had one another.

And just as they had shared the lottery winnings so now they would share the gloom and discomfort of not having any money for restaurant meals.

Mrs Peterborough cleared her throat and recited a limerick she had clearly just made up.

‘From one of these cards you must pick
But be warned, and beware, it’s a trick
You look for the Queen
But she’s not to be seen
For his hands are exceedingly quick.’

Mrs Caldicot wondered how she did it so quickly. It seemed that Mrs Peterborough could create silly little rhymes without any effort. She looked across at Mr Twist to see if he was offended. He wasn’t. Even he was smiling.

‘If we go round to the back of one of the big hotels we can probably persuade someone in the kitchen to give us some of their leftovers and unwanted food,’ said Mrs Merivale, who had once found herself abandoned in Rome by a film producer who had absconded with all the available funds, leaving the crew to fend for themselves. She therefore knew of what she spake.

Mr Merivale said that although he didn’t really like begging, he thought this was an excellent idea and, under the circumstances, entirely excusable.

‘One of us could go into a café and order a cup of something very cheap,’ suggested Mr Livingstone. ‘And while he’s in there he could fill his pockets with those little, wrapped sugar cubes they always have on the table in cafés and restaurants and then when he came out he could share out the sugar with everyone else.’

'I could probably get us some money,' said Mr Williams, speaking quietly to Mrs Caldicot. 'I still know one or two gallery owners in Paris. I could ask them to advance me some money on the sale of my photographs.'

Mrs Caldicot looked at him and smiled. 'No, Mr Williams,' she said quite firmly. 'You've helped us more than enough in the past. We must deal with this little problem ourselves.' She reached out and squeezed his arm. 'We'll sort things out,' she said. 'It'll be an adventure,' she added, and managed to sound as though she meant it.

'We could go to the British Embassy,' suggested Mrs Roberts. 'They ought to be able to help us. That's what they're there for, isn't it?'

The others immediately agreed that this was a splendid notion and it was generally agreed that they had no doubt that the British Embassy would have to help them out.

'Maybe they'll lend us some money and let us pay them back when we're back home,' said Ruth, who had tried to hide how she felt but was actually quite frightened.

And so off they went to the British Embassy.

Things did not go as well as they hoped.

After a lengthy wait a rather superior official in a smart suit, a white shirt and a boring looking tie told them that since they had their hotel booked and their return tickets arranged, there really wasn't anything that he could do.

'Can't you just lend us some money for meals?' asked Mrs Caldicot. 'We'll pay you back.'

'We don't lend people money,' said the official, rather sniffily. 'I suggest you telephone your bank in England and ask them to send some money for you to collect at a branch here in Paris. Alternatively, you could ask a friend or a relative to wire you some money. I think you will find that there is a Western Union office here in the city.'

Dismissed and feeling even lonelier and more abandoned than before, Mrs Caldicot and her friends stood in the street and tried to decide what to do next. Mrs Caldicot half wished she had accepted Mr Williams' offer to borrow some money from one of the gallery owners he knew. But she only half wished it.

'We could try the travel agency,' suggested Mr Livingstone. 'Aren't they supposed to have a representative here?'

Mrs Caldicot said she thought this was a splendid idea, probably even better than trying the British Embassy, and added that she didn't know why she didn't think of it herself. And so off they went, back to the hotel.

'Ah, tootle plip!' said Raphael when he saw them approaching.

'No, no,' said Mr Hewitt. 'Toodle pip is what we say instead of 'goodbye'. When you are greeting someone you say 'What ho! Good to see you old bean!''

'What ho! Good to see you old bean!' said Raphael.

'Splendid!' said Mr Hewitt.

Raphael who always looked pleased with himself managed to look even more pleased with himself.

Inside the hotel, Mrs Caldicot asked the receptionist if she could put them in touch with their travel agent representative. The receptionist found the number on a card pinned to the wall behind her and then made the call. When the phone was ringing, she handed the receiver to Mrs Caldicot.

'How did you lose your money?' asked the travel agent's representative when Mrs Caldicot had explained their problem.

Mrs Caldicot explained the sequence of events which had led to their loss.

The travel agency representative laughed.

'It's not funny,' said Mrs Caldicot sharply. 'We don't have any money left.'

'But your hotel is booked, isn't it? You've got somewhere to sleep? And you get your breakfast thrown in for free?'

'Yes.'

'So, what's the problem?'

'We don't have any money for other meals.'

'Then it was rather silly of you to lose all your money in a card game. And you still have your train tickets? You haven't lost those?'

'No, we still have the tickets.'

'Oh good. That's a relief. You'll be able to go home.' She said it rather nastily, unconcerned and indifferent to their plight.

Suddenly all Mrs Caldicot could hear was the dialling tone. The travel company representative had closed the connection.

'Can she help?' asked Mrs Torridge. 'Can the travel company lend us some money?'

'It would seem not,' admitted Mrs Caldicot who was a little shocked and extremely disappointed.

They stood around in the hotel lobby, wondering what to do next.

'We could do as the Embassy man suggested,' said Mr Roxdale. 'We could ask someone to wire us money to a bank.'

'There must be another way,' said Mrs Caldicot firmly. 'I don't know about the rest of you but I'm fed up with people putting us down. It'll seem like a defeat if we have to ask someone in the UK to send us some money.'

She knew that Jenkins would know how to send her money and he would do so happily and quickly. But she now very much wanted to deal with this problem without any outside help. The Embassy hadn't been much help. And the woman from the travel agency had been absolutely no help at all.

They were on their own and they would darned well deal with their problem themselves.

Chapter Fourteen

'Maybe we could earn some money ourselves,' suggested Mr Twist, very quietly. He spoke rather diffidently; still shaken and rather ashamed of himself.

They were still standing in the hotel lobby.

They all looked at Mr Twist.

'Did you see that violinist in the park?' he asked. 'Her violin case was half full with money.'

'We haven't got a violin or a violin case,' pointed out Mr Hewitt.

'No, but we have a flute, a banjo and a set of African bongo drums,' said Mr Livingstone. 'Mr Twist is absolutely right. We could earn the money we need.'

Now everyone looked at Mr Livingstone.

'My instruments,' he explained. 'The ones I brought with me. They're upstairs in my hotel room.'

'But only you can play any of them,' said Mrs Roberts.

'Anyone can play the banjo,' insisted Mr Livingstone. 'And all you need to play the bongo drums is a pair of hands.'

'We could be a band,' said Mrs Peterborough. 'I've always wanted to be in a band.'

'What shall we call ourselves?' asked Mrs Torridge.

'I don't think it matters what we call ourselves,' said Mr Hewitt. 'But can we make the sort of music that people will pay to listen to?'

'Of course we can,' said Mr Livingstone, with enough confidence for them all. Clearly delighted, he hurried upstairs to collect his instruments. 'Remember how well our little sing song went on the train?'

'But what will the rest of us do?' asked Ruth, who didn't think she could play the bongo drums and was pretty certain she wouldn't be able to play the banjo.

'I can play the comb and paper,' said Mr Roxdale, taking a pocket comb from his pocket. 'All I need is a bit of greaseproof paper or tissue paper. I used to be a wow at Christmas parties when I was a boy.'

He hurried away, heading for the kitchen and the friendly chef in the hope that he'd be able to beg a piece of suitable paper.

'Spoons!' said Mr Hewitt. 'I can play the spoons! I always found that soup spoons worked best.' And he hurried off after Mr Roxdale to borrow a pair of suitable soup spoons.

'What are the rest of us going to do?' asked Mrs Torridge.

'It looks as if one of us is going to be playing the banjo,' said Mrs Caldicot with a laugh. 'And one of us is going to be playing the bongo drums.'

'Oh I don't think I could manage either of those,' said Miss Nightingale.

'Nor me,' said Mrs Peterborough.

From the look on her face it was clear that Mrs Torridge wasn't keen on either instrument. She pointed out, quite sensibly, that she could hardly hold Mr Torridge and play an instrument.

'Maybe those who aren't playing musical instruments could sing,' suggested Mrs Caldicot. 'We could have a small choir. Bands always have a small group of singers.

'I wouldn't mind being a backing singer,' said Ruth. 'I could wear that blue dress I brought with me in case we got invited to any parties.' She looked down. She was wearing blue jeans, a blue jumper and her blue anorak. She liked blue. Apart from yellow it was her favourite colour. But she didn't like herself in yellow. She thought it made her look fat. She admitted to being curvy and rounded and didn't particularly object to being described as plump, which she thought sounded rather attractive, but she didn't want anyone to think of her as fat.

'But what on earth are we going to sing?' asked Mrs Torridge. 'I don't know any songs!'

'Of course you do!' said Mrs Caldicot. 'We were singing old music hall songs on the train coming over here.'

Moments later, Mr Hewitt and Mr Roxdale emerged from the kitchen.

Mr Roxdale had a piece of greaseproof paper wrapped around his comb and a very happy Mr Hewitt was clutching two shiny soup spoons and two jam jars, both of which appeared to be two thirds full of dried split peas.

‘What on earth are the jam jars for?’ asked Ruth.

‘Those are your rhythm shakers,’ explained Mr Hewitt. ‘Your home-made maracas!’ He shook the jars which, when shaken rhythmically, produced an almost musical percussion sound.

Ruth, delighted, took the two jars, one in each hand, and proceeded to practise with them.

‘I see we’ve already got the beginnings of a band!’ cried Mr Livingstone, coming down the stairs with far more energy than anyone had seen him travel for a long time. ‘Who’s on banjo?’

‘I’ll try,’ said Mrs Caldicot. ‘But you’ll have to show me what to do and if I can’t manage it then someone else will have to take over.’

‘I’ll just pop upstairs and change into something a bit more presentable,’ said Ruth who was now becoming quite excited at the prospect of being in a band – even if all the other members of the band were half a century older than her. Just wait until she told Denise that she’d been in a band which had performed in Paris! The best thing about Denise was that she never got jealous. On the contrary, she always got excited and genuinely delighted if anything remotely thrilling happened to her friend.

Had anything this exciting ever happened to anyone else they knew? Ruth thought not.

Clutching her home made maracas (she didn’t want to come back down and find that someone else had taken charge of them) the assistant housekeeper and band singer hurried upstairs.

‘I’ll have a go at playing the bongo drums,’ said Mrs Roberts.

‘What tunes are we going to perform?’ asked Mr Livingstone.

‘Mrs Caldicot suggested that we try some of those old music hall songs that we sang on the train,’ said Mrs Torridge.

‘Splendid idea!’ agreed Mr Livingstone.

‘So, where are we going to perform?’ asked Mrs Roberts.

‘The best place is the Place des Vosges,’ said Mr Williams. ‘But we could practise in the Tuileries Gardens, where we saw that girl violinist.’

‘We all need to get used to our instruments,’ Mr Livingstone pointed out. ‘And we need to decide which numbers we’re going to sing.’

‘How many numbers do you think we need?’ asked Mrs Torridge. ‘I hope it isn’t going to be too many.’

'Three will be plenty,' said Mr Livingstone. 'When we've performed the three, we can start again at the beginning.'

'Won't people get bored if we keep playing the same tunes?' asked Mrs Roberts.

'I don't think many people are going to stick around for more than three songs,' pointed out Mr Hewitt.

'Where's Ruthie gone?' asked Mrs Torridge suddenly.

'I think she popped upstairs to change,' said Mrs Caldicot, who was now making an effort to know where everyone was.

'As long as we don't go without her,' said Mrs Torridge.

'We won't,' promised Mrs Caldicot, who had absolutely no intention of going anywhere without her entire brood with her. She felt a particular responsibility for Ruth who was in some ways very grown up but in other ways seemed remarkably young even for an 18-year-old. Still, most young people seemed very young these days. First, she had noticed that policemen were getting younger. Then the doctors all looked as though they should still be at school flicking paper pellets about with rubber bands. Except that they all looked so serious that they had probably never flicked paper pellets about.

And so while they waited for Ruth to return, they discussed which traditional, old-fashioned music hall songs they knew, or knew well enough to give the impression that they knew them.

They eventually decided on these three:

Down at the Old Bull and Bush – made famous by Florrie Forde

Boiled Beef and Carrots – immortalised by Harry Champion

And

I Do Like to Be Beside the Seaside – which has been performed in a good many films, and which has for over a century been popular with British holidaymakers

Mr Hewitt said he thought that the third of these was rather inappropriate since they were nowhere near the seaside but Mr Livingstone pointed out that they weren't at the Old Bull and Bush either. And, moreover, come to that they weren't likely to be eating boiled beef and carrots at any time in the near future. As a result of Mr Livingstone's intervention, it was unanimously decided (including by Mr Hewitt) that Mr Hewitt's objection be forthwith overruled. Mr Livingstone also pointed out that those were the three old music hall songs for which he definitely remembered the lyrics and the tunes. And, as a double bonus they had easily memorable tunes and would doubtless be familiar to a good many tourists.

'I'll just write down the lyrics while we're waiting for Ruth,' said Mr Livingstone. He begged three pieces of hotel stationery from the receptionist and to his own surprise succeeded in scribbling some, at least, of the words to all three songs. He then managed to persuade the receptionist to make 20 photocopies of each sheet of paper, so that he had a few spares for each song.

'There you are,' he said, handing round the home-made song-sheets as they came out of the photocopier. 'Now no one has any excuse for not knowing the words!'

As the last piece of paper was handed out, they heard Ruth clattering down the stairs. Moments later she appeared.

The blue dress, made out of something very shimmery and sparkly, fit her perfectly. 'Not a straight line to be seen fore or aft,' said Mr Roxdale.

Ruth was certainly all curves and the dress made this abundantly clear. Her generous bosom, normally rather hidden under a jumper or an anorak or both, had suddenly leapt to the fore and was now unmistakeably there and undeniably feminine. There was cleavage in abundance. Ruth had somehow even found time to do something to her hair, which was now piled high on her head, and to complete the ensemble she wore long, blue, dangly earrings.

'Crumbs!' said Mr Hewitt.

'Wow!' said Mr Twist.

'Beautiful!' said Mr Williams.

'You look marvellous, dear!' said Mrs Caldicot.

'Blue really suits you!' said Mrs Torridge.

'I love the buttons!' said Mrs Peterborough who, as we now know, knew a good deal about buttons.

'You look good enough to eat!' said Mrs Merivale.

'Terrific! Absolutely terrific!' said Mr Merivale.

'Beautiful!' said Miss Nightingale. 'You're beautiful, my dear.'

'Crumbs!' said Mr Twist. 'You do look good.'

'Fantastic,' said Mr Williams who wished he had his camera with him.

Mrs Roberts gave Ruth a hug and Mr Livingstone tried to wolf whistle but discovered that somewhere along the line his whistle had upped and left him. He replaced the missing whistle with a round of applause which he managed quite well despite the rheumatoid arthritis in his fingers.

Ruth was delighted. Her audience might not perhaps have fitted the demographic profile of her preferred or chosen audience but they were her friends and their compliments meant a lot to her.

And so, all present and correct, they hurried out of the hotel, past Raphael the doorman (who remembered to say 'Tootle pop' as they passed by), and along to the Tuileries Gardens where they found a bench and some chairs and some of them sat down and some of them didn't and they tried to turn themselves into a band.

Chapter Fifteen

'How do I play this thing?' Mrs Caldicot asked Mr Livingstone, holding up the banjo and peering at it as though she were rather nervous that it might bite. 'Where do I blow?' She suddenly felt rather alarmed. She could not remember that she had ever played a musical instrument and she suddenly got rather cold feet. Then she remembered that when she was about seven she had played the recorder at school. Awful instrument, she remembered. She had hated it and not been any good at all at it. 'What if we make complete fools of ourselves?' she silently asked herself. 'So, what if we do?' she silently replied. 'Does it really matter? Does it matter at all? We don't know anyone in Paris? No one else will care. And it could be fun. It could make us some money for boat rides and food and so on. And whatever happens it will be an adventure.'

'You're kidding, aren't you?' said Mr Livingstone.

'Not a lot,' admitted Mrs Caldicot, suddenly shaken from her reverie. 'It's got strings so I assume it needs strumming rather than blowing. But although I did once try to play the guitar I never got very far with it.'

'It's a banjo,' explained Mr Livingstone patiently. 'Not a guitar or even a ukulele. And it's very easy to play. All you really have to do is strum.'

He showed her how to strum some simple tunes that made it sound as though she were playing the instrument.

'It sounds rather good,' said Miss Nightingale, appreciatively.

'It's very nice indeed,' agreed Mrs Peterborough. 'What's it called? Is it a guitar?'

'It does sound rather good, doesn't it?' said a genuinely surprised Mrs Caldicot. 'Mr Livingstone says it's called a banjo.'

Next, Mr Livingstone showed Mrs Roberts how to play the bongo drums. And to everyone's astonishment Mrs Roberts turned out to be tremendously adept.

'You're a natural,' said Mr Livingstone.

Mrs Roberts blushed with pride and carried on drumming.

'You're a natural,' whispered Mrs Caldicot, grinning at Mrs Roberts and giving her a nudge.

Meanwhile, Mr Livingstone, satisfied that he had a banjo player and a bongo drum player, had moved across to start teaching Ruth how to play the rhythm shakers which Mr Hewitt had made. He took one of the jam jars from her and shook it. He pulled a face and tried again.

'I could ask Jean-Jacques if he would like to join us,' Ruth said to Mrs Caldicot.

'Who is Jean-Jacques?' asked Mrs Caldicot, who didn't know that Ruth knew anyone in Paris, let alone someone called Jean-Jacques.'

'He was one of the waiters at that little party last night,' replied Ruth.

'I thought his name was Pierre,' said Mrs Caldicot. 'Wasn't he the one Mrs Peterborough wrote a poem about? The balding one.'

Mr Livingstone tried the other rhythm shaker and pulled another face. Well, actually it was the same face but he pulled it again.

'No, not that one,' said Ruth, now blushing. 'Jean-Jacques was the young good-looking one with the tattoo.'

'Ah!' said Mrs Caldicot, understanding. She didn't much fancy tattoos herself but she knew that young girls regarded them very seriously. And she knew that Ruth, like many young girls, had a welcome mat tacked onto her heart and a tendency to fall in love at first sight. She thought that when you were young and in a hurry this probably saved a good deal of time though it did have a tendency to produce a little pain and more than a few tears. Still, the presence of a revolving door in addition to a welcome mat, meant that the sadness and tears were usually soon replaced by fresh hope and new expectations.

Mrs Roberts was now really getting the hang of her bongo drums. 'Oh this is fun!' she cried out as she banged out a rather merry rhythm.

'I could text him,' said Ruth, rather eagerly.

'You have his number?'

'Oh yes. He wrote his number on a paper napkin for me.' She reached into her handbag and produced a carefully folded paper napkin. Written in lipstick it contained a telephone number and a large, red X.

Mr Livingstone was still shaking the jam jar full of dried split peas. He did not seem happy.

'Does he play any musical instruments?' asked Mrs Caldicot.

'Oh yes. He told me that he plays the accordion.'

'Won't he be working today?'

'He is a freelance and works in several bars and hotels. But he only works in the evenings. He said I could text him during the day time.'

'Well, if he doesn't mind,' said Mrs Caldicot, who was impressed that Ruth had managed to obtain all this information in such a short space of time. She had only seen the two of them talking together for a couple of moments. A thought suddenly occurred to her. 'But would he want to be paid to play his accordion?'

'Oh no, I don't think so,' said Ruth. 'Shall I ask him to meet us here?'

'Well, yes, I would think so. I rather suspect that we'll be here for a little while,' said Mrs Caldicot. She put the strap of Mr Livingstone's banjo around her neck and started to strum it as she had been instructed.

'Wow!' said Ruth, impressed. 'You make it sound like a banjo!'

'Do you mind if I take a few of these dried peas out of Ruth's maracas?' Mr Livingstone asked Mr Hewitt. 'I think we'd get a better sound with fewer peas.'

'Not at all! Remove as many as you think necessary,' replied Mr Hewitt, who was practising with his two soup spoons and proving to himself and everyone else that a skill acquired in childhood is a skill which is never truly lost. 'I just filled the jar up with peas. I knew it would need tuning but I thought it would be easier to take some out than to try to find an additional supply if we needed more.'

'Very wise,' agreed Mr Livingstone. 'Good thinking!' He unfastened the lid on the jar and poured some of the dried peas out into his hand. He put the peas into his jacket pocket. Half a dozen split peas spilt out onto the ground and were immediately eaten by three plump pigeons. Mr Livingstone then put the lid back onto the jar and tested the rhythm shaker. Satisfied, he made roughly the same adjustment to the second jam jar and then handed both back to Ruth when she had finished typing and sending her text message. He then gave her some basic instruction in how to turn her pea filled jam jars into musical instruments.

'Right,' said Mr Livingstone. 'We'd better try a run through of our first song. Let's try 'Down at the Old Bull and Bush'.

'What's a run through?' Mrs Roberts asked Mrs Caldicot, in a whisper.

'I think it's a sort of rehearsal,' Mrs Caldicot whispered back.

And so off they went with their first rehearsal.

The band was born.

Chapter Sixteen

To almost everyone's surprise the first run through was surprisingly successful. The exception to the doubters, was Mr Livingstone. He had long believed that faith can move mountains and that all you needed for this was enough faith and a small enough mountain.

Mr Livingstone led the way on his flute, Mrs Caldicot strummed the banjo, Mrs Roberts banged the bongo drums, Mr Hewitt did what he did with his spoons, Mr Roxdale made surprisingly musical sounds with his comb and greaseproof paper and the choir of Mrs Peterborough, Miss Nightingale, Mrs Torridge, Mr Twist, Mr Williams and the Merivales performed magnificently.

But none of them would have disagreed that the star of the show was Ruth.

Far from just being a backing singer, as she had at first imagined herself to be, she became the lead singer. She shook her jam jar maracas as one born to shake jam jar maracas and to her own surprise she turned out to have an excellent, slightly throaty voice – perfect for the rendition of music hall songs.

After their first run through of their triple programme of songs, the new band realised, with some astonishment, that they had acquired a considerable audience.

Moreover, when they finished their enthusiastic rendition of 'I Do Like to Be Beside the Seaside', they watched in astonishment as a number of members of the audience threw money down at their feet.

'We need something for people to throw money into,' said Mr Livingstone, who, it was generally agreed, had, by default, become the band's manager.

As he spoke, the musicians and singers were busy scouring the ground and collecting up the coins which had been tossed down. As they collected them, they handed them to Mrs Caldicot who popped them into her handbag.

'We certainly do,' said Mrs Torridge. 'My eyes aren't what they used to be and I've just picked up three bottle tops.'

She had, is must be admitted, been hampered in her search by her insistence on holding onto the bag containing Mr Torridge's ashes.

'Scrabbling around on the ground doesn't do my knees any good,' said Mr Hewitt. 'The ground is a lot further away than it used to be when I wasn't as old as I am now.'

'I should have brought my banjo case,' said Mr Livingstone. 'You can get a lot of loose change in a banjo case.'

'Use my hat!' said Mrs Torridge. She was wearing a wide brimmed straw hat which she removed and placed on the ground before them.

'Put a few coins into it,' said Mr Williams.

The others looked at him, puzzled.

'The buskers' version of salting the mine,' he explained. 'If people see money in the hat they'll be more likely to throw in coins of their own.'

Just then there was a squeal of delight and Ruth put down her jam jars and ran off towards a young man in blue jeans, a black, leather jacket and a strange little pork pie hat. He was carrying an accordion. With him was a considerably older man who was carrying a very large instrument case. When the two arrived, the older man opened his case and removed from it a complicated musical instrument which looked as though it were either a trumpet which had been overbuilt or a trombone which had been involved in a motor car accident and been uncomfortably compressed. Jean-Jacques gazed admiringly at Ruth who looked rather different in her blue dress. He introduced his father. 'This is my father, Monsieur Roche.'

Everyone said hello to Monsieur Roche who nodded and smiled and said hello to everyone.

Mrs Peterborough was driven to rhyme:

'A lovely young maiden called Ruth,
Fell in love with a handsome French youth.
'I may be a clot
But I love him a lot.'
And that, she declared, is the truth.'

Ruth blushed. Everyone else smiled. No one laughed. Not even a little bit. There was, however, applause for Mrs Peterborough.

Mr Hewitt, who had found a piece of cardboard blowing about the gardens, took out a pen and made a notice. He then placed it on a chair.

'This is Jean-Jacques,' said Ruth, introducing the young waiter, for he it was, to Mrs Caldicot and then to the rest of what used to be called a group of old people, but had by Ruth been described to her friend Denise as a travelling circus and which must now be properly described as a band. 'He's brought his accordion and his father, and his father has brought an instrument too. They both play for fun whenever they can.'

'That's a euphonium!' said Mr Livingstone, who knew about these things. 'I haven't seen one of those for years.' He paused for a moment and then laughed. 'I thought the Frenchies all just played the French horn!' Distracted by the joy of being a band leader, Mr Livingstone was at last enjoying his second trip to Paris.

Mrs Caldicot looked across at him and was delighted. Perhaps, she thought, just maybe, this enforced adventure might not turn out to be such a bad thing after all.

Ruth was delighted when Jean-Jacques kissed her, but a trifle disappointed that the kisses were all of the French-three-times-on-the-cheeks variety. Left cheek, right cheek, left cheek.

'Now you must kiss me the same,' said Jean-Jaques.

'Does it matter where you start?' asked Ruth.

'Not really,' said Jean-Jaques. 'Some people start with the right side. Others start with the left side. I always kiss left cheek, right cheek, left cheek.'

So Ruth kissed him three times on the cheeks, left cheek, right cheek, left cheek, and thought she had probably gone to heaven. One of her kisses missed his cheek slightly and landed on the corner of his mouth. He smiled at her and she thought he may have even winked a little.

Her joy was only slightly diminished still further when Jean-Jacques proceeded to kiss everyone else on the cheeks – including the men. His father then kissed her three times (left cheek, right cheek, left cheek) and then he too carried on to kiss everyone else. It would, she thought, take her a while to become accustomed to this Parisian kissing business.

'What music are we playing?' asked Jean-Jacques, who seemed to Mrs Caldicot so speak much better English than all the people she had met who claimed to speak perfect English.

Mrs Caldicot explained that they were playing three old time British music hall songs and Mr Livingstone handed both Jean-

Jacques and his father copies of the song sheets the receptionist at the hotel had photocopied for him.

Jean-Jacques and his father looked puzzled as they read through the song sheets.

'We'll play a run through of 'Down at the Old Bull and Bush' and you join in whenever you feel like it,' said Mr Livingstone.

For the first time they played it, both Jean-Jacques and his father simply stared in quiet astonishment. But then they gradually got the hang of things and joined in, playing the tunes and singing the songs as well as they could. There was no doubt that the band sounded considerably more meaty (as Mr Livingstone put it) with the addition of an accordion and a euphonium. This was old-fashioned British Music Hall as it had never before been played.

Most of those who came within earshot were fascinated.

And within earshot was a goodly distance for a flute, a banjo, a set of bongo drums, an accordion and a euphonium, not to mention a pair of soup spoons, a pair of matching maracas and a comb and greaseproof paper, produce a noticeable sound.

And then, of course, there was the choir: Mrs Peterborough, Miss Nightingale, Mrs Torridge, Mr Twist, the Merivales and Ruth (with her home-made maracas).

Even without the sound of the instruments it would have been difficult to miss the choir. Rarely, if ever, have those three old songs been rendered with more enthusiasm. They may not have always been in tune and occasionally one or two of the words were missed but there was no shortage of gusto. If they had anything in abundance it was gusto.

A large group of small French schoolchildren, all holding onto a rope fitted with little, wooden handles, stopped and watched one whole song before their teachers urged them on to some pre-ordained destination. One of the teachers made what looked like a very small donation. A group of British old aged pensioners stood and listened through the band's entire repertoire and joined in the singing of songs they had once known well and were now obliged to dig out of their memories. They made generous donations to Mrs Peterborough's hat, some making donations in euros and others throwing in what they would doubtless have described as 'proper money'.

Fascinated American tourists gave generously (one put in a ten dollar note), and courting couples from all nations contributed smiles and money.

Two women wearing tailored suits and sensible shoes stalked past as though the band were not there at all. Mr Roxdale said they looked like horses who had been ridden hard across country and now wanted nothing more than a long drink and a bucket of oat mash. They sniffed snootily as though they were walking past a septic tank with the wind blowing in their direction. They were the only ones to take no notice of the band and the music it was playing.

Altogether, dozens of tourists stopped and took photographs, short films and selfies.

'I think we're going to be famous!' said Mrs Peterborough to her friend Miss Nightingale.

'We were filmed by some Japanese tourists!' said Ruth who had posed several times for camera wielding Orientals. Three times during one twenty minute period, gentlemen of slightly advanced years had asked for her name, which she had given without hesitation. She wondered if she might perhaps end up with an online fan club. That would certainly be something to tell Denise and everyone else back home.

With Mrs Torridge's straw hat in place, it was clear to passers-by that Mrs Caldicot and her chums were busking. And as they continued to play their admittedly limited repertoire, the band received a steady stream of contributions. As the moving crowd of tourists, dog walkers and others wandering through the park, tossed their coins into Mrs Torridge's straw hat, it was soon clear that before long they would have raised enough money to pay for a meal each.

'My hat has never seen so much money!' said Mrs Torridge proudly.

'I don't think I've ever seen so much money!' said Mr Livingstone who, like most of the band, did not think he had ever felt happier in his life.

The money they had earned through their music was, in some strange way, not like any other money they had ever earned. In some indefinable way, this money was more 'real' than money received in a wage packet or as interest on an investment. And it was money they had earned through necessity. They had dragged themselves out of a situation in which many would have despaired. And they had done it together, as a small community. Every single one of them had contributed in their own way.

'We'll have to keep an eye on that hat,' said Mr Hewitt. 'We don't want it getting ideas and running off with all the loot!'

'Oh my hat would never run off,' said Mrs Torridge firmly. 'It's a very well brought up piece of millinery.'

'Should we be sharing the money with your young waiter and his father?' Mrs Caldicot asked Ruth.

'Oh no,' said Ruth. 'I told him what had happened and they don't want any of the money. They're happy to help out. They enjoy playing.'

'When did you tell them what had happened?' asked Mrs Caldicot.

'When I texted,' said Ruth.

'You did all that in a text?' said Mrs Caldicot, astonished.

'Oh yes,' said Ruth.

'Golly,' said Mrs Caldicot, who was quietly astonished. She had a mobile telephone and had, quite recently, begun to master the art of sending text messages. But it still took her a quarter of an hour to send something to Jenkins. And there were invariably some complications in the creation of the message. So, for example, the message 'What would you like for dinner?' would usually come out as something more like 'Ygat xi8ld 9nu jikd eoq dhmnds'. Capital letters and punctuation were both a foreign country to her.

The band played its entire repertoire several times, and twice Mrs Caldicot had to empty Mrs Torridge's straw hat because it was becoming overfull with money. There were coins of all denominations and the more enthusiastic music lovers had put euro notes into the hat.

Chapter Seventeen

Eventually, Jean-Jacques announced that he and his father, both waiters who worked only in the evenings, had to leave to go to work.

'Are we doing this again tomorrow?' asked Jean-Jacques after he and his father had completed a round of kissing (left cheek, right cheek, left cheek and then left cheek, right cheek, left cheek) to mark their departure.

If meeting and leaving always take this long then I'm surprised anything ever gets done in France, thought Mrs Caldicot. It took the best part of ten minutes for Jean-Jacques and his father to kiss everyone and for the band members to reciprocate. 'We certainly are,' she said. 'We have enough money for dinner tonight, but if we don't play again then we won't have any money for meals tomorrow.'

'May we join you when you play again?' asked Jean-Jacques.

'We'd all be delighted!' said Mrs Caldicot. 'And I think it is fair to say that Ruth would be very delighted.'

Ruth, who was standing next to Mrs Caldicot, blushed in a very dainty, girlish sort of way and gave Mrs Caldicot a gentle nudge as though pretending to tell her off.

'Are you sure you won't take any of this money?' asked Mrs Caldicot, pointing to the cash which was now safely stashed in her handbag.

'Oh no, no!' said Jean-Jacques. 'My father and I love to play music. And you need the money to replace what was taken from you by bad people.' He paused. 'May I make a suggestion?'

'Of course!'

'You would perhaps do better for the money if you play in the Places des Vosges. The acoustics are very good and people go there deliberately to listen to the music played by buskers. There are always bands and choirs and soloists there.'

'The Place des Vosges! That's the place Mr Williams recommended!' remembered Mrs Caldicot. 'Is it far?'

'No, it's not too far. We can come to your hotel and then show you how to get there. We can, if you like walk from the hotel to save money on the Metro fares. It's a pleasant walk through the Marais – the old quarter of Paris.'

Mrs Caldicot said that this was extremely kind of them.

'We should be at the Place des Vosges by 11.00 a.m.,' said Jean-Jacques. 'That should enable us to select a good spot. We can play in the cloisters. The sound is very good there and if it rains neither we nor the people listening won't get in the slightest bit wet.'

Mrs Caldicot said she thought this sounded marvellous and they arranged to see one another at 10.00 a.m. sharp the following morning. 'Oh, one thing occurred to me,' she said, as an afterthought, 'do we need a licence of any kind to play music in Paris?'

Jean-Jacques grinned and shrugged his shoulders. 'Technically, you do,' he said. 'But…' He shrugged again.

'Oh dear. I don't like that 'but'? What happens if the police catch us?'

'Usually, you run!' said Jean-Jacques. He looked around and his eyes settled first on Mrs Torridge with her walking frame and then on Mr Livingstone who was rubbing his knee and finally over the rest of the band. None of them looked like people you'd put your money on if it came to a chase. He frowned and shrugged again. 'But perhaps not so much of the running…'

'Will the police put us in jail if they catch us?' asked Mrs Caldicot.

'No, no,' said Jean-Jacques. 'They would not dare!' His father, who had been listening, shrugged in that way the French do when faced with something patently absurd and then slowly headed off with his euphonium, now packed away safely in its case. 'Anyway,' said Jean-Jacques, 'it is easy for you – you give your hotel address and then you go back to England. What can they do?'

Slightly reassured, but nevertheless nervous at the prospect of having to make a run for it across the Channel, Mrs Caldicot thanked him again. She wondered what Jenkins would say if she arrived back home with a busload of gendarmes in hot pursuit.

And then Jean-Jacques, about to follow his father, turned back and spoke to Ruth. 'May I kiss you?' he asked with surprisingly old-fashioned politeness.

'Yes, of course!' said a rather surprised Ruth, expecting another trio of French on-the-cheek kisses.

But it was not a kiss on the cheek.

And a couple of minutes later, when she emerged from the embrace breathless and panting slightly, her hair a little dishevelled, Ruth was blushing bright red.

With a final wave, Jean-Jacques, clutching his heavy accordion, hurried away to catch up his father.

Mrs Peterborough delayed not a moment.

'Our Ruth had two jars filled with peas
With these she made music with ease.
A handsome young waiter
Decided to date her
And gave her a kiss and a squeeze.'

Ruth was still waving goodbye with one hand when with the other she reached into her bag and pulled out her mobile phone.

Now she really did have something exciting to tell Denise.

As they headed back towards their hotel, Mrs Caldicot remembered the notice that Mr Hewitt had made with a piece of abandoned cardboard. The notice was still on the chair where it had been placed. She picked it up to read, and this is what it said: 'Newly formed Band. Please Give Generously to Pay for Music Lessons.'

Mrs Caldicot, laughing, picked up the sign and popped it into a waste bin.

They had, she thought, done quite well without any music lessons.

Chapter Eighteen

After taking their instruments back to their hotel, the band (for this is how they now saw themselves) had dinner at a pleasant, traditional café a few hundred yards away. To the especial delight of Mrs Torridge and Mr Livingstone, it involved nothing more than a gentle shuffle down the road and along a narrow, slightly out of the way side street.

It was a café which Jean-Jacques and his father had recommended.

It was not an establishment where they worked but it was a place where they sometimes ate.

'I can't think of a better recommendation than that!' said Mrs Merivale.

It was not a café which catered for tourists and, indeed, there was no tourist menu advertised outside. The food, however, was excellent and very reasonably priced.

At the conclusion of the meal, Mr Twist, who was still in charge of their finances paid the bill with several handfuls of coins – the money which they had earned and which had been thrown into Mrs Bartholomew's hat.

(In view of recent events, Mr Twist had asked to be excused from all fiscal responsibilities but it was unanimously decided that he was the best person for the job and Mrs Caldicot in particular had insisted that he continue in the role as Band Accountant. She had, when they returned to the hotel, handed over to him all the day's takings. There was far too much cash to fit into his money belt and so he had stuffed the notes into his wallet and the coins into every available pocket.)

The waiter huffed and puffed a good deal as he counted the money but his demeanour improved when he discovered that he had been given a more than acceptable gratuity.

'I do appreciate your trust in allowing me to continue to look after our finances,' Mr Twist said to Mrs Caldicot as they all strolled back to their hotel.

'You've always done a wonderful job for us,' said Mrs Caldicot. 'I have never been any good at accounts and you've managed the money back at the house very well. I really don't know what any of us would have done without you. The day when you first came to stay with us was a Red Letter day as far as I am concerned.'

'But…' began Mr Twist. He was, at times, a man given to emotion and he could feel tears in his eyes. There had been many bad times in his life and now he felt that he was enjoying the best of times. He swallowed. 'I still feel so bad that I lost all our money. It was a stupid and indefensibly reckless thing to do.'

'It was stupid and it was reckless,' agreed Mrs Caldicot who saw no point in denying these obvious truths. 'But your intentions were good. And I think we can safely say that naivety led you astray.' She looked at him and smiled. 'We will leave it at that. And I don't think we need mention it ever again.'

'Thank you,' said a contrite and grateful Mr Twist.

'And there is one thing you did for which we will, I think, always be grateful,' said Mrs Caldicot.

Puzzled, Mr Twist looked at her. He did not think he was a stupid man (although, of course, he would never deny that he was liable to moments of idiocy, as illustrated by his recent debacle) but he really didn't understand what she was talking about.

'Have you forgotten?' asked Mrs Caldicot, with a big smile.

'Forgotten what?'

'It was your idea that we should start a band and go busking to raise money,' said Mrs Caldicot.

Mr Twist thought and remembered that indeed he had been the one to suggest that they might try earning some money by playing music. He remembered seeing the young girl violinist with all the money in her violin case.

'Yes, I suppose it was,' he agreed. 'But we only had to do that because…'

Mrs Caldicot held up a hand to stop him. 'Your idea has brought us all together, given everyone a sense of purpose and added a great deal of unexpected joy to our holiday,' she said.

Mr Twist hesitated for a moment. 'Do you really think so?'

'I'm sure of it,' said Mrs Caldicot with a big smile. 'I really don't think I've ever seen everyone quite so happy. I rather suspect that Mr Livingstone, in particular, is very pleased that our money was lost. And I know that everyone is excited about tomorrow – wondering how we'll get on playing music in the Place des Voges; wondering how much money we'll earn and so on.' She laughed. 'I certainly didn't think I'd ever see the day when I'd be strumming a banjo in a public park in the middle of Paris!'

'So,' said Mr Twist hesitantly, 'do you think the good idea perhaps cancels out at least some of my silliness in losing our money in the park?'

'I think it does,' said Mrs Caldicot. 'In fact, I'm sure it does.'

'Nothing like that will ever happen again,' promised Mr Twist.

'Oh I know that,' said Mrs Caldicot, who did.

And Mr Twist felt happier and more at peace than he had felt for some time.

When they arrived back at the doorstep of their hotel, the doorman, Raphael was still standing there.

'He doesn't do much but he does it for long hours,' muttered Mr Hewitt to Mr Roxdale.

'What ho, old beans!' Raphael cried, pleased as Punch with his new command of idiomatic English.

'What ho, Raphael!' replied everyone, almost as a chorus.

Mr Hewitt and Mr Roxdale, who wanted to speak to Raphael, hung behind for a moment after the rest had gone into the hotel.

'You're not still teaching him your brand of English are you?' Mrs Caldicot asked them when they finally sauntered in.

'Just a few words to help him communicate more effectively with tourists,' said Mr Hewitt.

'Oh dear,' said Mrs Caldicot. 'I don't think I want to know what you've been teaching him.'

'All good fun!' said Mr Roxdale.

'All part of the entente cordiale!' said Mr Hewitt.

And then, quite exhausted by the excitement of what had been a long day, they all went up to bed.

And their dreams were coloured and enlivened by indelible memories of their impromptu concert in the Tuileries Gardens

Chapter Nineteen

At five minutes to ten the following morning, Paris's most newly formed band was standing in the lobby of its hotel. There had been no trashing of hotel rooms and no television sets had been thrown out of bedroom windows. Drug use had been confined to the taking of modest quantities of medicinal drugs prescribed, variously, for conditions such as high blood pressure, heart problems and arthritis. There had been no illegal drug use and although Mr Hewitt and Mr Roxdale had enjoyed medicinal tots of brandy (obtained from the mini bar in their rooms) there had been very little alcohol consumption.

The band members were ready and waiting, and although the massed tourist industry of Paris might well have been disappointed if they had been aware of this, they were far, far more excited than if they had been about to visit the Louvre, ascend the Eiffel Tower or wander up and down the Champs-Élysées.

Mr Livingstone's banjo was in its case because it was generally thought that it would, with all due respect to Mrs Bartholomew's hat, be a more suitable receptacle into which their audience could toss their donations. Mr Twist had some loose change left over from the day before and he was prepared to use this to 'seed' the banjo case when they started playing.

Ruth, who was wearing her blue dress again, had somehow managed to find some blue paper, and she had stuck this to the outside of her jam jar rhythm shakers so that they looked less like jam jars and considerably more like musical instruments.

Mr Hewitt had his spoons in his jacket pocket and Mr Roxdale had his comb and paper tucked into the breast pocket of his jacket, and since they were hardly laden down with the weight of their instruments, they had each offered to carry one of Mrs Roberts's borrowed bongo drums, for which she was duly grateful.

Mrs Peterborough, Miss Nightingale and Mrs Torridge were constantly clearing their throats and reciting the words of the three songs they had learned. Miss Nightingale was still having some trouble with one or two of the lines of 'I Do Like to Be Beside the Seaside'. The bit which was proving a challenge was the couplet at the end of the third verse which went: 'I do like to stroll along the Prom, Prom, Prom! Where the brass bands play, 'Tiddely-om-pom-pom!'

The singers all had their song sheets with them but said they very much hoped to be able to manage without them.

Mrs Torridge had brought along her hat and the plastic carrier bag in which Mr Torridge was now accustomed to travel. She had announced that her hat was still available to serve as a coin repository if there proved to be any problem with Mr Livingstone's banjo case. When she was excited, and raring to go, Mrs Torridge trembled a little and her walking frame made a sort of drumming sound on whatever ground lay beneath it. The result, not entirely unpleasant, was rather akin to the sound a powerful petrol engine motor car makes when it is idling. The casual observer can tell that there is power there; virtually dormant for the moment but waiting to be unleashed. Those who knew Mrs Torridge well were all aware, when they heard the sound of her walking frame a-throbbing, that, at the boom of the starting pistol, she would be off and on her way.

Miss Nightingale had brought along part of her collection of woollen bobble hats: one in red, one in blue, one in green and one in white. She said that she, Mrs Peterborough and Mrs Torridge were going to wear their bobble hats when they sang. They reported to Mrs Caldicot, however, that there was what could only be described as a logistical problem. Miss Nightingale had brought four bobble hats with her and there were only three suitable heads upon which to place the hats since neither Mrs Merivale nor Ruth were fond of woolly hats.

Mrs Torridge had expressed a preference for the red hat and Mrs Peterborough said she thought she fancied the white one. That left Miss Nightingale with a choice and Miss Nightingale was not good with making choices; not when they were important choices.

'Which do you think I should wear?' she asked Mrs Caldicot, to whom she was accustomed to turn when faced with any dilemma of some magnitude. 'Which would be smarter? Which would be more appropriate?'

Mrs Caldicot knew, from long experience, that Miss Nightingale needed someone she trusted to make the decision for her and so she took the time to consider the dilemma.

'I think,' she said, after some thought,' 'I think you should definitely wear the red one. For one thing the red suits your complexion and for another thing if the three of you are wearing red, white and blue hats the combination will have a distinctly patriotic look. They will be British colours, of course, but the French will also approve because their flag had the same three colours and so any French people who see your hats will probably assume you are all celebrating the French tricolour. The green hat can be held in reserve, lest some calamity befall one of the other hats.'

Miss Nightingale was delighted by this verdict.

As they awaited the arrival of Jean-Jacques and his father, there was an almost palpable air of excitement in the hotel lobby.

'Odds bodkins!' said Raphael, the doorman when Mrs Caldicot finally stepped foot outside the hotel, to see if Jean-Jacques and his father were anywhere in sight. 'May I crave a boon?'

Mrs Caldicot, who had been closely followed by the rest of the band, looked at Raphael and then glanced at Mr Hewitt and Mr Roxdale who were, like a couple of schoolboys, struggling to suppress their giggles.

'You may crave a boon,' said Mrs Caldicot graciously.

'Thank you, ma'am,' said Raphael. 'Can I fix you people up a taxi? A minibus, perhaps? The hotel coach is available if you need it. Very reasonable prices.'

'We're walking, thank you,' said Mrs Caldicot.

'Shanks's pony,' said Mr Roxdale.

'Or mare,' said Mr Hewitt. 'I've heard it described as Shanks's mare.'

'Who was Shanks?' asked Mr Livingstone. 'I've always wondered about that.'

'Some people say there was no Mr Shank,' said Mr Williams. 'When I was nothing but a lad, my mother told me she thought the phrase referred to the fact that the lower leg is sometimes referred to as the shank. I suspect I was a curious boy; always asking daft questions. I must have been a bit of a nightmare.'

Raphael, who was trying to follow this conversation, now looked thoroughly confused.

'Oh,' said a disappointed Mr Livingstone. 'That's a bit disappointing.'

'I agree,' said Mr Williams. 'But there may be another explanation. My father told me that Mr Shank was an 18th century vicar who couldn't afford a pony and had to walk everywhere round his village. So when he wanted to visit his parishioners or pop down to the local inn for a glass of mead he used what the villagers called Shank's pony. I always preferred that explanation though I never knew whether my Dad made it up or not. He used to do that to try to confuse me. It used to get me into terrible trouble at school. I remember being put into detention for insisting that Lawrence of Arabia wrote *Lady Chatterly's Lover.*'

'What the devil was mead?' asked Mr Roxdale. 'I've always wondered about that.'

'Some sort of alcoholic drink made with honey,' said Mr Williams who sometimes felt slightly embarrassed at the amount of entirely useless information he had accumulated over the years.

'Did your Dad tell you that?' asked Mr Roxdale.

'No, I think it's pretty reliable information,' said Mr Williams. 'My mother told me that. She didn't usually make things up.'

'Here come our accordion and euphonium players!' said Mr Merivale. He pointed down the street where it could be seen that Jean-Jacques and Monsieur Roche, his father, were approaching. Monsieur Roche, who was dressed ready for work, was wearing a pair of black trousers, a white shirt and a black waistcoat. He was carrying his jacket and his euphonium case. Jean-Jacques was wearing a pair of pale blue chinos and a blue button down shirt. He was wearing his accordion and did not have its case. He afterwards explained to Ruth that the case was nearly as heavy as the accordion.

Ruth, whose heart had been beating so loudly that she felt sure everyone around must have been able to hear it, hesitated for a moment but then succumbed and ran forward to meet the young accordionist. Clearly pleased to see Ruth, he kissed her, just once and not on the cheeks, and she would have doubtless blushed an even brighter shade of red had it been possible.

'I like that dress very much,' Jean-Jacques said to Ruth.

'It's the only decent dress I brought with me,' said Ruth, apologetically. 'The only other things I've got are jumpers and trousers and an anorak and they don't seem the right things to wear; not for performing in public.'

'I love the dress,' said Jean-Jacques. 'My father apologises but he has to work this afternoon. He will play with us for an hour or so and then leave. This is why he is wearing his clothes for waiting.'

'It's very kind of him to come at all,' said Mrs Caldicot.

'No, no, it is a thrill for us to play with you. My father loves playing and does so whenever he can. And I too love playing music.'

'Right!' said Mrs Caldicot, adopting again her role as wagon master. 'Shall we hit the road?'

And so, after murmurings of enthusiasm and a few notes of approval from Mr Livingstones's flute, they set off towards the Places des Vosges.

'Tally ho!' cried Raphael as they left. 'The games afeet, eh?'

'The games afoot!' chorused everyone in reply.

'Have you been singing for long?' Jean-Jacques asked Ruth. They were, of course, walking together.

Ruth laughed. 'Only since yesterday. And you? How long have you been playing the accordion?'

'Since I was a little boy. I was given a small instrument for Christmas when I was six. I wanted a drum set but my parents decided an accordion was more sensible since we lived in a small apartment with very thin walls. When I was 12, my uncle died and he left me this instrument. I could hardly lift it but I was very proud to have it and I have been playing it ever since. It is my most treasured possession.'

It took them an hour to walk from their hotel to the Places des Vosges.

'This is the best way to see the city,' Jean-Jacques said to Ruth. 'The buses and the coaches are too fast. When you walk you can look into the shops, and see the buildings and get the real feeling of the streets. Many people who visit Paris walk very little. It is a shame.'

They walked along the Rue Saint Honore, home of some of the most expensive boutiques in the world; shops where rich tourists can spend a small fortune on a pair of gloves and a large fortune on a handbag. Both Mrs Peterborough and Mrs Torridge gasped when they saw the prices.

They walked past small, private art galleries selling works of art by modern painters. Mrs Torridge said the stuff which was hanging on their walls, or on display in their windows, looked no better than the sort of pictures, done with brightly coloured crayons, which loving mums stick on their refrigerators. Mr Livingstone said he thought it was the artists, not the pictures, who ought to be hanging somewhere.

The galleries were mostly empty of buyers. No one seemed to be looking at anything. Each gallery contained but a single occupant: a willowy, snooty looking woman of a certain age and the willowy, snooty looking women appeared to spend their time making phone calls or looking at their emails. How, wondered Mrs Caldicot, did the gallery owners make a living? She asked Mr Williams who explained that the galleries sold things to professional dealers who put what they bought into storage, in the hope of eventually making a profit when they resold, or rented it out to banks and corporations who displayed what they had rented in their lobbies and boardrooms. In the end, he said, most of the saleable stuff ended up in auction rooms in New York where it was bought by professional dealers who put what they bought into storage, in the hope of eventually making a profit when they resold, or temporarily rented it out to banks and corporations who displayed what they had rented in their lobbies and boardrooms.

Mrs Caldicot said none of this made a lot of sense. Mr Williams said it didn't have to make sense as long as it made money.

They strolled past the entrance to the magnificent Palais Royal, a former royal palace which was, back in the 18th century the centre of Parisian social life, full of famous cafes; its covered walkways a favourite showground for aristocrats and courtesans. They took a moment to peer in through the gates. The lime trees were already in leaf and nannies were taking babies and small children for their morning constitutionals. A man in a beige raincoat was feeding small pieces of bread to the sparrows; the chattering birds were gathered on his arms and head. Half a dozen tourists were eating sandwiches, bought from a nearby shop. Loving couples were strolling arm in arm; hoping for a little early spring sunshine. Everyone was hoping for a little early spring sunshine.

They hurried past the extraordinary Pompidou Cultural Centre, an infamously inside out building with its pipes and ducts on display instead of being hidden away beneath the structure's fabric. Sadly, the once famous building now appeared rather seedy and grubby looking. It had apparently become a magnet for the homeless, the dispossessed and the canine. They hurried past the Pompidou and then wandered at a more leisurely pace through the Marais, an area full of delicatessen shops and one of the oldest parts of Paris.

(It should, perhaps, be admitted that 'hurried' is a comparative term. None of the party, other than Jean-Jacques and his father, was of an athletic nature and it was never likely that any speed records were likely to be broken. Mrs Torridge, relying on her walking frame, and Mr Livingstone, with a right knee and a left hip that were long past their best, both had a top speed which was not far removed from 'very slow'.)

They stopped for a moment to admire the packed window of a delicatessen which had several types of snail for sale.

Mrs Torridge, Miss Nightingale and Mrs Peterborough screwed up their noses at the sight. Mrs Peterborough found a limerick irresistible.

There was a young lady from Wales
Who liked chocolates filled up with snails
She said: 'They taste funny'
But cost not much money
'Cus I buy the damned things in the sales'.

The streets were full of young people and Mr Roxdale couldn't help noticing that a good number of them were young girls in their 20s.

'I wish I were younger,' he said to Mr Hewitt, and held his chest as though he were having a heart attack. He grinned.

'I remember reading about a bloke called Clemenceau,' said Mr Hewitt. 'He was the French Prime Minister during the First World War. When he was 80-years-old, he was walking down the Champs-Élysées with a friend when a pretty girl walked past. Clemenceau stopped and admired the young girl. 'Oh to be 70 again,' he said as she strolled past.'

Mr Roxdale laughed.

Jean-Jacques explained to Ruth and to the others which buildings were famous because of the people who had lived in them. He pointed out landmarks they would have missed. He showed them places where important things had happened. He drew their attention to long-established shops and important statues and told them the history of the streets along which they were walking.

On their way through the streets of Paris, Mrs Roberts popped into several shops trying to buy postage stamps to put on her postcards. Her search was, however, always in vain. The shops she visited all sold postcards but none of them sold the stamps to stick on them.

'Are you looking for anything in particular?' Monsieur Roche asked her after her third disappointment.

'Just some stamps for my postcards,' explained Mrs Roberts, holding up her small sheaf of postcards to illustrate her point.

'Ah, you will need a main Post Office,' said Monsieur Roche. 'They will sell stamps.'

'Do you know where I can find a Post Office?' she asked him.

Monsieur Roche thought for a while and then shook his head sadly. 'No. I don't think there is one around here, I'm afraid. There is a Post Office in the Rue Etienne Marcel and there is one in the Rue La Boetie – they are the nearest.'

'Are they anywhere near where we are going?'

Monsieur Roche shook his head. 'I am afraid not.' He thought again. 'There is one in the Rues des Francs Bourgeois but sadly we have passed that one. And there is one in the Rue Castex but I think it is closed now for something or other.' He shrugged, using his shoulders, arms and hands. 'I am so sorry. Do you have something important to post?'

'Oh no, just some postcards,' said Mrs Roberts, with a smile. 'I just need some stamps for my postcards. But there's no hurry. They can wait.'

Chapter Twenty

As they threaded their way along a narrow and busy street called Rue des Francs Bourgeois, Mrs Caldicot was approached by an elegantly dressed woman and a tall, distinguished looking man. They both appeared to be in their fifties and looked as though they had just stepped out from the pages of Vogue magazine. She was wearing a simple, white, polka dotted dress (with the dots in blue) and blue shoes which looked as though they had spent their short lives walking on carpet rather than hard pavements. He wore a lime green, linen jacket, sharply creased white linen trousers, two-tone shoes (in brown and white) and an immaculate Panama hat.

She was carrying a handbag of a blue that matched her shoes and dress. The bag looked just about big enough to carry a single lipstick and half a packet of paper hankies. If you'd tried to cram a mobile phone in as well, the bag probably wouldn't have closed properly.

He was carrying an expensive looking movie camera.

Mrs Caldicot, who had been walking for nearly an hour felt downright grubby in comparison. She was wearing her favourite red dress but it had not travelled well and it was now criss-crossed with creases. ('Don't worry about it,' said Ruth, when Mrs Caldicot had shared her fear that she looked as though she had slept in the dress for a week, 'the creased look is very fashionable at the moment. People are buying clothes that have loads of creases put into them before they're sold.' Mrs Caldicot, who had never had much interest in fashion, had not gained much comfort from this well-meant reassurance.)

'Sorry to bother you, ma'am,' said the tall man, touching his hat with the forefinger of his right hand, 'but do you speak English?' He spoke in an accent which did not disguise the fact that he was an American.

'It's the only language I do speak,' said Mrs Caldicot, with a smile.

'That's marvellous,' said the man, with a sigh of relief. 'My wife and I are looking for the Place des Vosges. You don't happen to know where it is, do you?'

'Follow us!' said Mrs Caldicot. 'That's where we're going.'

The smartly dressed American couple walked alongside Mrs Caldicot. The pavement was narrow and people all around were walking along the road. Fortunately, there was very little traffic and what there was moved along at little more than a brisk walking pace.

'I'm Calvin and this is my wife Josephine,' said the man. 'We're on a tour of Europe.'

'This is our third week over here,' said Josephine. She had a strong Southern accent which Mrs Caldicot found enormously charming. 'We've been to England, Wales and Scotland and now we're in France for the week. You must excuse me, I do look a sight I'm sure. The airline lost several of our bags and we're having to make do with what we have.'

'Are you folk all travelling together?' asked Calvin. He turned and looked back at the rather long line of elderly Britons who were wandering along in Mrs Caldicot's wake.

'Yes we are,' said Mrs Caldicot. She looked around. Miss Nightingale waved. Mrs Caldicot waved back. 'I'd introduce you to everyone but it'll take rather a long time.'

'Are you some sort of band?' asked Calvin. 'I notice that you and one or two of your colleagues are carrying musical instruments.

'Well we are a sort of band,' agreed Mrs Caldicot. 'We're hoping to play in the Place des Vosges – to earn some money!' She held up the banjo case she was carrying. 'This is a banjo,' she said. 'I borrowed it from Mr Livingstone. He plays the flute.'

'You're on a European Tour?'

Mrs Caldicot laughed. 'Sort of! Actually, I suppose you could describe it as our inaugural world tour!'

'Where are you performing? Is there a hall in the Place des Vosges?'

'Oh no, we're performing in the street. We're hoping to find a nice, quiet piece of pavement where we can play.'

'Oh my,' said Josephine. 'Is that allowed? Playing in the street?'

'To be honest I'm not entirely sure,' admitted Mrs Caldicot. 'But if we are going to eat today we don't have a lot of choice!'

'How long have you been playing the banjo?' asked Calvin.

'Just since yesterday. I don't really play it. I just sort of strum it and hope it doesn't sound too bad.

'Has your band been together a long time?' asked Calvin, who seemed slightly bewildered by Mrs Caldicot's reply, but who was far too well-mannered to say anything.

'Since yesterday afternoon,' replied Mrs Caldicot.

It was clear that neither Calvin nor Josephine quite knew what to say to this.

'What sort of music do you play?' asked Calvin after a long silence.

'British Music Hall songs,' said Mrs Caldicot. 'We only know three songs so we do them in rotation. Our repertoire consists of 'Down at the Old Bull and Bush', 'I Do Like to Be Beside the Seaside' and 'Boiled Beef and Carrots'. I'm afraid that we don't do requests and if people don't like those three songs then we can't do much about it.'

'I don't think I know any of those songs,' said Josephine. She looked at her husband who shook his head.

'They're very old and very old-fashioned British music hall songs,' explained Mrs Caldicot. 'But we're all old-fashioned and British and most of us are very old so they seemed appropriate.'

'So, if you aren't experienced musicians, do you mind my asking how you came to form a band?' asked Josephine.

Mrs Caldicot did her best to explain. It took some time.

'Oh that's awful,' said Josephine.

'But your response to your vicissitudes is rather wonderful,' said Calvin. 'Is that what they call the British bulldog spirit?'

'I rather suppose it is,' agreed Mrs Caldicot.

'Do you mind if I film you when you start playing?' asked Calvin. He lifted up the camera he was carrying.

'Not at all!' agreed Mrs Caldicot. 'Some people filmed us yesterday but they only had mobile phones. Your camera looks very professional.'

'We like to keep a record of our travels,' explained Calvin. 'Neither of us has been to Europe before.' He took some film of Mrs Caldicot and then of the rest of the band as they walked along the street. Three French boys on bicycles stopped and stared when they saw Calvin's camera. They pedalled slowly and meandered along just behind Mrs Caldicot. Two girls of about the same age as the

French boys came out of a side street, paused for a second or two, grinned at each other and then followed the boys. A mackerel tabby cat with a piece chewed out of one ear jumped down from a window sill and joined the procession.

Chapter Twenty One

Eventually, almost exactly at eleven o'clock in the morning, they arrived at the magnificent and historic Place des Vosges: the oldest square in Paris.

Monsieur Roche explained to them all that the Place des Vosges was, back in the 17th and 18th centuries, the place for the fashionable to have their homes. The posh people of Paris might have taken their pleasures in the Palais Royale but they kept their children and their servants in the Place des Vosges.

'The Place des Vosges is an exact square,' explained the knowledgeable Monsieur Roche who pointed out that Victor Hugo, author of *The Hunchback of Notre-Dame* and *Les Miserables*, lived in No 6 Place des Vosges, which had been turned into a museum in his honour. He also told them that in the 17th century, Cardinal Richelieu also lived in the Place des Vosges.

Richelieu, claimed Monsieur Roche, was unfairly portrayed as the Chief Baddy in Alexandre Dumas's novel *The Three Musketeers* (and in all the films based on the book). The waiter said he felt that Dumas had treated Richelieu badly, and that he had perhaps done this simply because he needed an enemy against whom Athos, Porthos, Aramis and D'Artagnan could pit their wits and their swords. Monsieur Roche said that it was rather sad that most French people had forgotten that Richelieu established the first orderly government in France, founded the Academie Francaise and rebuilt the Sorbonne University.

They came into the Place des Vosges rather suddenly and quite unexpectedly.

One minute they were walking along a fairly ordinary, narrow street ('Is it much further?' asked Mr Roxdale who quietly confessed to Mr Hewitt that, as Mrs Torridge had once said, he didn't think his legs had got much more 'walk' in them) and the next moment, to their astonishment, they were standing in the most wonderful square in Paris. William Wordsworth Esquire, poet and spring flower aficionado, dawdling round a corner and finding himself unexpectedly faced with a host of golden daffodils, all making pretty, little curtseys in a pleasant spring breeze, could not have been more delighted.

Around the perimeter stood grand houses; all joined to dominate the small garden or park in the middle of the square. Beautiful trees were just coming into leaf and already there were people sitting on the benches. Every park and garden in Paris is liberally supplied with benches or chairs or both and the park in the Place des Vosges was no exception.

Some of those on the benches were reading a newspaper, a magazine or a book; some were chatting; some were eating sandwiches; some were simply enjoying the peace and the spring sunshine in a Parisian oasis. There was a children's play area hidden behind some bushes in the small park and the members of the band (for they now definitely thought of themselves as a band) could hear, but not see, children laughing and squealing with delight.

The square and the park were full of linden trees, which the British usually refer to as lime trees, and as a result, the whole area was full of the distinctive aroma associated with the genus tilia. Mr Hewitt, who had an observant eye and an encyclopaedic knowledge about things botanical, remarked to Mr Roxdale that the streets and parks of Paris seemed to be dominated by just three types of tree: lime trees, horse chestnut trees and plane trees.

'We must first find a place to play,' said Monsieur Roche. 'We must hurry. This is a favourite square with musicians.'

He led the way into the cloisters which ran around the square, tucked in the shade underneath the grand houses. The others in the party, some of them now rather weary after what had been a long journey, tottered after him. Mrs Torridge, in particular, had struggled to keep up and her knees were giving her a lot of trouble. She had to pause and lean on her walking frame every dozen yards or so. Mrs Caldicot had several times offered to carry the bag containing Mr Torridge but Mrs Torridge had declined gracefully and with thanks and insisted that she was perfectly capable of carrying her husband while using her walking frame. Once or twice Mrs Peterborough joined her in leaning on the frame though naturally this meant that they had to move in step. Despite the difficulty she was having, Mrs Torridge had steadfastly refused to give in. When Mrs Caldicot had suggested that she and Mr Livingstone, who also suffered with terrible arthritis, should take a taxi, Mrs Torridge had insisted that she would 'get where they were going under her own steam, thank you very much for asking'. Mr Livingstone had simply growled something under his breath and had seemed offended at the suggestion that he might need to travel in a motor vehicle, particularly since the chances were high that the vehicle would be driven by a French person.

As Mrs Caldicot and the rest of the band followed Monsieur Roche around the square, Calvin continued to film them. He, of course, was followed by his wife. And the three boys and two girls were still following him. As was the cat whose curiosity was now thoroughly aroused and who seemed convinced that if he kept going, something good would come out of it. Six Chinese tourists, three men and three women, saw what was by now a considerable crowd and joined the parade.

The Chinese men were all wearing identical grey suits which were made out of something shiny and synthetic which looked a little like silk but probably wasn't since there wasn't an unwanted crease anywhere in sight. The Chinese women were all wearing smart, red dresses which appeared to be made out of the same material. All six had camera phones seemingly fixed to their eyes and they filmed Calvin and everything that Calvin filmed.

In one corner of the square, a jazz band was playing. There were three saxophonists, a keyboard player, playing a small, portable keyboard, a violinist and two guitar players. In another corner there were two folk singers, both with guitars. They seemed to be singing their own compositions. And in a third corner two women with large, stringed instruments were comfortably settled playing something which Mr Williams said was by Bach.

Each group of performers had their own small audience. Others, walking past, would stop for a few moments to listen.

The odd thing was that due to the unique acoustics of the cloisters, and their extent, the quality of the sound each group of performers made was perfect and as you stood listening to one set of performers you could not hear the others. It wasn't difficult to see why musicians, and those wanting to listen to good music in the open air, flocked to the Place des Vosges.

'I've never known how to tell the difference,' whispered Mrs Caldicot to Mr Livingstone, who was glad they had slowed down a bit since his right knee had been playing up a good deal. 'Are those cellos or double bases?'

'Those are cellos,' said Mr Livingstone, whispering his reply. 'The double bass is slightly bigger than the cello. Cello players always sit down with their instrument between their legs. Musicians playing a bass can play it sitting down but they usually prefer to stand. It's a big instrument, a bit hefty to carry around.'

'Thank you,' whispered Mrs Caldicot who still didn't think she'd be able to tell the difference but wasn't going to worry about it.

Monsieur Roche found that there was one corner of the square unoccupied and Mrs Caldicot and the band immediately established their occupancy of the space. Their small area was soon alive with the sound of players tuning up their instruments and singers doing what singers do to exercise their vocal chords. Mrs Roberts gave her bongo drums some healthy exercise, Jean-Jacques loosened up his accordion and Mrs Caldicot strummed her banjo rather hesitantly. It took her a moment or two to get into the rhythm of the thing.

'Before we start, I think everyone should have a little something to eat,' said Mrs Merivale. She opened a large carrier bag and displayed a huge pile of croissants, each one carefully wrapped in a paper napkin. 'Just to keep us all going until lunchtime.'

'Where on earth did you get all those?' asked Mrs Caldicot with a beaming smile.

'From the breakfast buffet,' replied Mrs Merivale. 'Mr Merivale and I collected them and wrapped them.' She paused. 'Well, after all, when we're in England Mr Merivale and I are usually in charge of comestibles,' she explained.

It was generally agreed that Mr and Mrs Merivale were heroes. Mrs Peterborough said that they should definitely be recognised in the next New Year's honours list and Miss Nightingale seconded the suggestion.

'Where's Mr Hewitt?' asked Mrs Caldicot, suddenly noticing that the band's spoons player was missing. She took a croissant from Mrs Merivale's huge bag, thanked her and took a bite. A few flakes of pastry fluttered down to the pavement and a sparrow which just happened to be passing swooped down and collected its lunch.

‘He’s over in the park in the middle of the square,’ said Mr Twist, taking a large bite from his croissant. A second sparrow hopped over, took a large crumb and flew off to enjoy it in privacy. ‘He and Mr Roxdale spotted some weeds which they thought they needed attending to.’

‘Well, we need them here!’ said Mrs Caldicot. ‘You couldn’t have the Beatles performing on stage while Ringo was off doing a little dead-heading! And how would it look if the Rolling Stones were doing a concert at the Royal Albert Hall and Mick Jagger suddenly looked round and said ‘Where’s Keith?’ and someone said ‘Oh, he’s just popped across the road to do a bit of weeding in Hyde Park.’

The flaky croissant crumbs were now falling like light rain, and a battalion of sparrows were hopping about snatching them up and taking them away. There were baby sparrows to be fed in nests secreted deep within the bushes of the small park in the centre of the square.

Ruth giggled and hurried across the road to fetch back the spoons player and the comb and paper specialist and five minutes later the entire band was, as Mr Williams put it, ‘ready to rock and roll’.

‘But we’re not performing rock and roll, are we?’ murmured a slightly puzzled Mrs Roberts. ‘I thought we were doing old-fashioned music hall numbers.’

‘It’s just an expression,’ explained Mr Williams. ‘Lots of people say it when they’re about to start work.’

‘Oh, right,’ said Mrs Roberts. ‘Let’s rock and roll then!’ She tried to wiggle her hips a little, a la Elvis Presley, but winced and didn’t do it again.

Mr Roxdale and Mr Hewitt put away their gardening tools, stuffing them into their jacket pockets, and prepared themselves for the band’s first performance of the day. Mr Roxdale checked the paper wrapped around his comb and Mr Hewitt polished his spoons because, as he said to Mr Roxdale, ‘a good spoons player always likes to sparkle’.

Chapter Twenty Two

Within minutes the band, which had not yet begun to play, had a sizeable audience. Many of those who were watching were a little intrigued by the size of the band but, perhaps, more fascinated by their average age and the nature of some of the instruments. Not every Parisian music lover is au fait with the playing of the spoons or the comb and paper and not many of those waiting for the music to start had ever seen a band which also included a flute, a banjo, an accordion, a euphonium, a pair of bongo drums and a girl in a blue dress shaking what looked suspiciously like two jam jars filled with dried peas.

And when the band did start to play (counted into 'I Do Like to Be Beside the Seaside' by Mr Livingstone, waving his flute like a conductor wielding his baton) the impact was immediate.

There was no doubt that the band was doing something new and different; the musicians were performing with unrivalled enthusiasm and with great passion (in some cases, it must be admitted, with more passion than skill or natural talent).

And, of course, they were, on average, about 50 years older than the other musicians performing in the cloisters of the Place des Vosges that day. It is not often that you can wander through the streets of Paris and suddenly find yourself watching and listening to a group of septuagenarians, octogenarians and nonagenarians performing 'Down at the Old Bull and Bush' as though their lives depended upon it (which, in a way, I suppose they did).

How many times do Parisians, or visitors to Paris, have a chance to see a man with a trowel, a fork and a dibber sticking out of his jacket pocket playing a pair of soup spoons and, moreover, creating something which definitely sounded like a tune?

How many times do music lovers get to see a rhythm section consisting of a shapely, 18-year-old girl shaking two jam jars filled with dried peas and a middle aged woman playing the bongo drums as though her life depended on it?

It was a rare sight.

The sound the band made, augmented with great skill by the feisty accordion playing of Jean-Jacques and the solid sound of his father's euphonium, was quite probably unique in the history of Parisian street music.

The streets, parks, arcades and colonnades of the City of Light have seen countless soloists; violinists, cellists, saxophonists, keyboard players, guitarists, singers (accompanied by taped backing tracks), trumpet players and players of just about every other instrument imaginable. The colonnades and parks and tourist high-spots have always resounded to the sound of small orchestras, string quartets, jazz bands, blues bands, pop groups and folk groups from all around the world. Residents and visitors have always been able to find music on the streets and in the parks of Paris.

But had anyone ever heard old British music hall favourites on the streets of the French capital?

Judging by the reactions of the audience which the band collected, it seemed likely that they had not.

Calvin filmed the band as an entity and then filmed each individual performer. Josephine, his wife, stood beside him drawing his attention to players whom she thought he should film next. The six Chinese tourists were still alternately filming the band and Calvin. The three boys and bicycles, and the two girls who were following them, had now been joined by five military cadets and a traffic warden. The mackerel tabby cat had thought about having a sparrow for lunch but he had decided against it. He had wandered off into the park for a while and had returned.

A coachload of elderly tourists from the Netherlands joined the crowd. The Dutch tourists nearly all wore beige and all had plastic name badges pinned to their clothes. A dozen young French tourists in their twenties joined them. Most of these newcomers carried extendable selfie sticks and spent most of their time taking pictures of themselves with the band in the background. To do this they had to face away from the performers. It seemed to Mrs Caldicot to be a strange way to go through life; viewing the world over your shoulder and back to front.

And still the audience grew and grew.

The Dutch tourists, most of whom were female, seemed fascinated by Mr Hewitt's skill with his spoons. One stood less than a yard away from him filming his hands and the spoons and looking at him most admiringly.

After just a quarter of an hour, and one performance of the three songs which they knew, Mrs Caldicot and her band had acquired an audience so large that it not only filled their corner of the cloistered walkway but spread out across the road and into the park in the centre of the square.

Other musicians, whose own aficionados had wandered off to see what all the excitement was about, had put down their instruments and wandered along the square to see what was going on.

Mr Livingstone's banjo case had been almost filled with coins, and not a few notes, and it seemed to Mrs Caldicot that if things carried on at this rate then they need no longer worry about their not being able to afford to eat decent meals that day.

As they paused for a short break, before beginning their next rendition of their three selected songs, a tired looking man in a scruffy suit which may have once been expensive but which had seen a lot of action and had not been cleaned for a long time, wandered over to Mrs Caldicot. He looked to be in his 40s. He had a cigarette dangling from his lower lip. Mrs Caldicot thought he reminded her of someone but she couldn't think who it was.

'Are you in charge?' he asked. As he spoke, the cigarette, which seemed able to defy gravity, bobbed up and down. He spoke English with a heavy French accent, and Mrs Caldicot thought this was fair enough since he was definitely French. Mrs Caldicot suddenly remembered that he reminded her of Serge Gainsborough, the famous French entertainer and song writer.

'Oh no,' said Mrs Caldicot, who knew enough about life to know that it is never a good thing to admit to being in charge.

'I run a club in Montparnasse,' he said, taking no notice of Mrs Caldicot's denial for he also knew enough about life to know that it is never a good thing to admit to being in charge and, in addition, also knew enough to be able to tell who was in charge even when they said they weren't. 'I'm always looking for acts that are a bit different.'

'Oh!' said a startled Mrs Caldicot.

'I can't pay you much,' he said. 'But give me a ring and we can fix up a few gigs.' He handed Mrs Caldicot a business card. 'My number is on the back, together with my email address.'

He then wandered off, his cigarette spilling ash down his suit.

'We've collected just over 150 euros!' whispered Mr Twist to Mrs Caldicot. 'Where shall I put all the coins? There's too much to leave in the banjo case. And I'm worried about pick pockets.'

'Can you put the coins in your pockets?'

'There are too many!' said Mr Twist.

'Just spread the money around,' suggested Mrs Caldicot. 'Give everyone with pockets some of the money to look after. That way no one will be able to steal the money for our next meal!'

'Open your handbag!' said Mr Livingstone, who was helping Mr Twist distribute the accumulated funds.

Mrs Caldicot, who had put her handbag on the ground between her feet, bent down and picked it up. She opened it and Mr Livingstone scooped in a handful of mixed coins. He then wandered off, distributing the takings among the rest of the band.

'Did you really only start the band yesterday?' Josephine asked Mrs Caldicot.

Her husband was still filming. He had now crossed the road and was standing in the park, filming the crowd which had collected and which was waiting patiently for the band to start playing again.

'We did,' said Mrs Caldicot.

'That's amazing!' said Josephine.

'We really didn't have a choice,' explained Mrs Caldicot. 'The man at the Embassy didn't seem terribly excited by our predicament and the woman from the travel agency wasn't in the slightest bit interested. So if we wanted to eat we had to make some money.'

'What else are you going to play?' asked Josephine.

'I'm afraid we have to play the same songs again,' said Mrs Caldicot apologetically. 'Those are the only three songs we know.'

'That's fine,' said Josephine. 'I don't think the audience will mind. Besides, your crowd is changing all the time.' She nodded towards the crowd which was watching them. The six Chinese people had gone and so too had the coachload of people from the Netherlands. They had been replaced by a small army of Japanese tourists and a dozen stout German men, some of whom were unwisely wearing traditional lederhosen and looking rather sticky and uncomfortable. The boys on the bicycles had gone. And, inevitably, so too had the girls who had followed them. The cat was now asleep on a window sill. Despite the losses, there had been a steady increase in the size of their audience.

'Is this a good crowd?' Mrs Caldicot asked Monsieur Roche.

'I have never seen so many people watching one group of musicians,' said Monsieur Roche. 'You are a big, big hit. No one has ever heard anything like it before.' He grinned. 'And I suspect that maybe these songs are not often accompanied by music played on an accordion and a euphonium.'

Mrs Caldicot laughed. 'I suspect you're right,' she agreed. She told him about the man in the scruffy suit and showed him the man's visiting card. 'Is he real, do you think?'

Monsieur Roche looked at the visiting card. 'Oh yes,' he said. 'This is a real person. He owns a big club in Montparnasse. It is a very popular club. He is known for always having something different on his stage. I had heard that he comes to the Place des Vosges occasionally looking for new acts.'

'Crumbs!' said Mrs Caldicot.

'Pardon?' said Monsieur Roche. 'Why is 'crumbs'?'

'Sorry,' said Mrs Caldicot. 'It's just an English expression. It means gosh, golly or my word.'

'Ah,' nodded Monsieur Roche. 'I understand. It is quite a tribute to be invited to play at this club.' He wandered back to where he had been standing when playing his euphonium.

And a few moments later, Mr Livingstone waved his flute and the band once more moved effortlessly into 'Down at the Old Bull and Bush'.'

'We didn't start with this one last time, did we?' shouted Mr Twist.

'No,' agreed Mr Livingstone with a shake of his head. 'I thought we'd do our three songs in a different order. Break the routine.' He laughed. 'It might convince people that we're playing something new.'

'Good idea,' agreed Mr Twist. He couldn't remember when he'd last had this much fun. He looked across at Miss Nightingale, Mrs Peterborough, Mrs Torridge and Mrs Merivale. They were all glowing. There was no other word for it. They were glowing. And Ruth, dear young Ruth, had blossomed into a butterfly in a blue dress.

The audience was not so easily convinced that the band was playing something new.

Quite a few of them had been standing listening for half an hour or more and they recognised the tune which they heard and they realised that they now knew the words. And, as a result, several hundred people, many of whom did not speak a word of English, now joined in singing 'Down at the Old Bull and Bush'.

'I never thought I'd be standing in a posh bit of Paris playing 'Down at the Old Bull and Bush' on the spoons with a crowd of Japanese and German tourists singing along,' said Mr Hewitt to Mr Roxdale.

Mr Roxdale, who was busy playing the comb and paper, could not reply.

Mr Hewitt tried a tricky, little manoeuvre which involved him playing the spoons on and around his left elbow. He was really getting into this. It was, he supposed, like swimming or riding a bicycle. You never really forget how. Effortlessly, he moved the spoons down to his right knee. 'Oh, I'm cooking with gas now,' he thought to himself.

Mrs Caldicot, who was now getting the hang of the banjo and rather enjoying it, noticed that Calvin and Josephine were now also singing 'Down at the Old Bull and Bush'. Calvin had temporarily put down his camera. Mrs Caldicot looked around. The band members were lost in the wonder of the moment. She couldn't remember ever seeing them have quite such a good time. Actually, she couldn't remember ever seeing any group of people have such a good time.

It was true that they might not have won any prizes in a music competition but they were playing their dream with a real passion, and passion rules all.

They were living a dream none of them had ever dreamt, or even imagined of dreaming, and the joy and the glory of the moment were untarnished by bad memories or unfulfilled hopes.

Mrs Caldicot wondered what Mr Hawksmoor, the manager of the Twilight Years Rest Home would think if he could see them now. She wondered what Derek and Veronica, her son and daughter-in-law, would think if they could see her. The pair had dumped her into a nursing home because they said she couldn't look after herself.

'Well, just look at me now!' she thought to herself and she felt at least six inches taller.

No, that was wrong.

A foot taller.

Chapter Twenty Three

At twenty past two, Mrs Torridge announced that if she didn't sit down she would fall down. She, Mrs Peterborough and Miss Nightingale had all been resting on Mrs Torridge's walking frame and although their enthusiasm and spirit had taken them through their tiredness they were now well into the foothills of complete exhaustion.

Everyone agreed that they needed a rest, a sit down and a cup of something refreshing. Exactly what it was didn't matter.

Oh, and it was generally agreed that something to eat would be welcome too.

'Banging these bongo drums had made my hands sore and my wrists ache,' said Mrs Roberts.

'I hit my funny bone with my spoons twenty minutes ago and my left arm has been tingling since then,' said Mr Hewitt. 'Have we made enough lolly for a cup of tea each?'

Mr Roxdale said he desperately needed some new greaseproof paper to wrap round his comb since the original piece of paper had now gone rather soggy and wasn't working properly.

Mr Twist, Mr Williams and both the Merivales agreed that they too were getting a little weary and would not turn down a chance to turn some of their earnings into suitable comestibles and liquid refreshments.

And even Ruth, who was young enough not to know what exhausted really meant, was ready for a break. Her throat was quite sore and she'd done a lot of jiggling about and she felt sort of, well, quite sticky. She was thirsty and fairly hungry and, more importantly, she wondered if she could ask someone to take a picture of her with Jean-Jacques. She could then send it to Denise. Damn it, she would send it to everyone whose address she had in her telephone. She wondered if Jean-Jacques would put his arm around her for the photograph. Maybe if she sort of snuggled in close and sort of just sort of put her arm around him he would respond by sort of putting his arm around her and then maybe he'd even sort of kiss her for the photo.

'Gosh I could eat a horse!' said Mr Hewitt.

'If you eat anything with meat in it then you probably will,' said Mr Merivale. 'The French eat a lot of horses.'

Mr Hewitt pulled a face. He quite liked horses, even when they stopped to eat a mouthful of daisies and came in last; and he didn't want to eat one. 'An omelette would do just fine,' he said.

Mr Twist scooped the remaining money from the banjo case and poured a couple of handfuls of cash into Mrs Caldicot's already rather full handbag. He then poured more coins into Mrs Roberts' handbag, and then into every available handbag and pocket.

'How much did we make?' Mrs Caldicot asked him.

'I've no idea!' replied Mr Twist. 'But enough to buy us all a meal now and another meal this evening. I saw one of those Chinese fellows put a twenty euro note into the banjo case. And there were several five and ten euro notes in there.'

'My word!' said Mrs Caldicot.

'We are going to take a break now?' said Monsieur Roche.

'We're going to have a meal and something to drink,' said Mrs Caldicot. 'Where do you recommend?'

'Not the cafés here in the Place des Vosges,' said Monsieur Roche, pulling a disapproving face. 'They are very expensive and very crowded – full of tourists. I can take you to a good café where the locals eat.'

'Is it far?' asked Mrs Caldicot.

'Three minutes,' said Monsieur Roche with a smile. 'Maybe four if we walk slowly.'

'I think we'll be walking slowly,' said Mrs Caldicot.

'But when I have taken you to the café I have to leave you,' said Monsieur Roche. 'I have to go to work.'

'You aren't going to eat with us?'

'I'm afraid not. But Jean-Jacques will stay I think. He doesn't have to work until this evening.' Monsieur Roche paused and looked around. 'Ah,' he said. 'I think he has a good reason to stay.'

Mrs Caldicot looked in the same direction.

Jean-Jacques and Ruth were having their photograph taken by Mr Williams. They had their arms around each other and Ruth looked as though she might well burst with the excitement of it all.

'Now give her a kiss,' Mr Williams said to Jean-Jacques.

And the danger of Ruth bursting went up a notch to Red Alert.

'We haven't added up the money yet,' said Mrs Caldicot. 'Can I just give you a handful as your share?'

'No, no, no!' said Monsieur Roche, holding up a hand and backing away. 'I don't want any money. It has been a pleasure to play with you.'

'But you're not even having lunch with us!'

'It has been a marvellous experience,' said Monsieur Roche. 'And I now have added three new songs to my repertoire. I have for many years had some knowledge of French music hall songs – the sort played by Mistinguett and Edith Piaf. But I did not know much of British Music Hall. As we walked here this morning Mr Livingstone told me that our French music hall was derived from your British music hall theatres and I can see that. But with some exceptions, such as the American Josephine Baker, many of our music hall songs tend to be rather sad and romantic whereas your British songs seem so jolly; they are very bright and bouncy. Mr Livingstone has promised to send me a CD containing a variety of other British music hall songs. I hope he will do that for me. I would appreciate it very much.'

'If he has said he will do that then I know he will do it,' said Mrs Caldicot. 'Together he and I will put together a package of old music hall songs then you can perhaps learn more of them. We will send you CDs and sheet music.'

'I would like that very much indeed,' said Monsieur Roche. 'You must let me know the cost.'

'No, no, no!' said Mrs Caldicot. 'This will be our present to you; our 'thank you' to you for bringing your euphonium and playing with us!'

As the band slowly wandered away, rather weary and in some cases not a little hoarse, a xylophone player wheeled his instrument into the corner they were vacating. Sadly for him, the band's audience drifted off and the xylophone player, who had been hoping to inherit the band's crowd, had to earn his own supporters.

Monsieur Roche led the band through an archway and along a narrow passageway and they found themselves in a large square garden which was surrounded by high walls. A violinist was playing 'Non, je ne regrette rien', one of the songs made famous by Edith

Piaf. The acoustics of the garden gave the violin a beautiful, mystical quality. Monsieur Roche led them across the garden and then through an archway at the other end. Within a minute or so they were in the broad and busy street of St Antoine, a continuation of the Rue de Rivoli. And within another two minutes they were outside a simple and unprepossessing café. The café was busy and there did not seem to be room for them all.

'Wait here a moment,' said Monsieur Roche. 'I will have a word with the proprietor and see if he can find tables for you.'

Monsieur Roche disappeared into the café and came out almost immediately accompanied by a large man wearing a huge moustache and a white apron which reached down below his knees. He was wearing other things, of course, but the moustache and the apron were the only two items which caught the eye.

'There is a big room upstairs,' said Monsieur Roche. 'Usually it is only opened in the evenings when there are more customers but this is Monsieur Ricard, the proprietor, and he will open it for you especially. There is plenty of room and the food here is excellent and very well priced.'

Monsieur Ricard greeted Mrs Caldicot with a handshake and escorted her and her companions to the stairs leading up to his upstairs dining room.

'I will send up a waiter in a moment,' he told them. 'Make yourselves comfortable.'

Monsieur Roche was absolutely right. The food was excellent, the service fast, efficient and friendly and the prices very reasonable.

'We would never have found this place by ourselves,' said Josephine, who, with her husband was sitting at a table with Mrs Caldicot and Mr Twist.

'Nor would we!' said Mrs Caldicot.

'How did you meet that wonderful man with the euphonium?' asked Calvin. 'It was a euphonium wasn't it?'

'Yes, it was a euphonium and how we met him is a long story,' said Mrs Caldicot. 'Monsieur Roche, the euphonium player, is the father of Jean-Jacques who is the accordionist. Jean-Jacques is a waiter who was working at our hotel and he took something of a fancy to our Ruth who, conveniently, took quite a shine to him. Things sort of happened from there!'

'Ruth is your daughter?'

'No, I'm afraid not,' said Mrs Caldicot. 'Nor is she my granddaughter I'm afraid! I would be proud of her if she were, but she works with us. We all live together in what used to be a nursing home, and Ruth helps with the cleaning and the shopping and things like that.'

'A sort of housekeeper?'

'Exactly!' replied Mrs Caldicot. 'Her official title is 'Assistant Housekeeper'. Now tell me about you two. All I know is that you're on a long holiday in Europe!'

'Until three months ago we owned a publishing company,' explained Josephine. 'We published half a dozen local newspapers. But the internet has damaged our sales and our advertising and when we received an offer to buy us out we thought it would be a good time to retire.'

'The buyers aren't closing any of the papers so no one is being made redundant,' said Calvin, for whom this was clearly important. 'But they're setting up websites and publishing them in conjunction with digital stuff that to be honest I really don't understand.'

'And the film making? Is that a hobby or something more serious?'

'Oh, that's just a hobby,' replied Calvin.

'Don't listen to him,' said Josephine. 'He's being over-modest. He's been making short documentary films for years. It started out as a hobby but for a few years now he's been selling the films to a local television station. And now the people who've bought the newspapers say they want to put some of the films on their websites. It's quite exciting because they're a big national company with lots of online viewers.'

'That's wonderful!' said Mrs Caldicot who thought it was.

'So, unless you object, my little film about your band could be seen by quite a lot of people!' said Calvin.

'Oh we don't object,' said Mrs Caldicot. 'We'd all be thrilled. Perhaps you could send us a copy of your film when it's finished? Or tell us where we can watch it.'

Calvin promised to send Mrs Caldicot a copy of his film.

And then, to Mrs Caldicot's utter astonishment, Calvin and Josephine insisted on paying the entire restaurant bill.

'Oh you can't,' protested Mrs Caldicot. 'It's far too much!'

'We absolutely insist,' said Calvin. 'You've given us the best day of our vacation.' Calvin patted his camera. 'And you've provided us with some marvellous footage to take back home.'

'You can use your earnings to pay for a good meal this evening!' said Josephine.

Mrs Caldicot stood up, banged her spoon on her saucer, and told the rest of the band that Calvin and Josephine had insisted on paying for their meal. There was much cheering and many cries of appreciation. Mr Williams insisted on a chorus of 'For They Are Jolly Good Fellows' and Mr Livingstone called for three cheers. Calvin and Josephine both blushed but Mrs Caldicot could tell they were secretly delighted.

Chapter Twenty Four

When Calvin and Josephine had left, Mr Twist counted the money they had taken in the Place des Vosges.

It came to an astonishing 287 euros and 25 centimes. There was also £7.20 in English money and $15 dollars in American money.

'Does this mean that we won't be playing music this afternoon?' asked Mrs Torridge.

There was silence as everyone waited to hear what Mrs Caldicot had to say.

'I suppose it does,' said Mrs Caldicot. 'We've certainly got enough money for our meal this evening.'

'But what are we going to do instead?' demanded Mrs Torridge who sounded terribly disappointed. 'Mr Torridge will be quite devastated if there is to be no more singing.'

'Yes,' said Mrs Peterborough. 'And he won't be the only one.'

'What are we going to do instead?' asked Miss Nightingale plaintively. 'I like singing our songs,' she said quietly. She seemed close to tears.

'I suppose we could go up the Eiffel Tower,' said Mrs Merivale, with about as much enthusiasm as she might have suggested that they find a dentist and all have a little, light root canal work. 'They say there's a good view of the city from up at the top.'

The suggestion was greeted with silence.

'Would you like to go up the Eiffel Tower?' asked Mrs Caldicot.

Mrs Merivale didn't have to think about it. 'Not especially,' she admitted with a bit of a shrug.

'We could go on a river boat,' suggested Mr Merivale. 'Cruise up and down for an hour or two and, er, look at the river bank.'

This idea was greeted with as much enthusiasm as the suggestion that they ascend the Eiffel Tower had been received.

Suggestions from Mr Twist, Mr Roxdale and Mrs Caldicot were also greeted without much enthusiasm from anyone, including those who had made the suggestions.

No one, it seemed, was terribly excited by the prospect of doing any of the usual touristy things.

Ideas which had filled them with excitement when they had been discussed back home were now regarded as dull and rather boring.

They sat for a while, finishing off the remains of the bottles of wine which Calvin and Josephine had bought to accompany their excellent luncheon. Mr Williams found a slice of baguette which he started nibbling. Everyone stared at the tablecloth because everyone was thinking the same thing but did not like to say it.

Everyone, that is, except Ruth and Jean-Jacques who held hands and looked at each other. They were happy to stay where they were for ever more.

'Are we sure there's enough money in the kitty to pay for any of these trips and to pay for tonight's meal?' asked Mr Hewitt.

It was the first small step in the direction they all wanted to go.

'Have we enough money to pay for lunch tomorrow?' asked Mrs Roberts.

'It could be raining tomorrow,' Mr Roxdale pointed out. 'We won't be able to earn any money if it's raining.'

'Mr Roxdale is right,' said Mr Williams. 'If we don't have enough money to buy a meal tomorrow then we'll be in a bit of trouble.'

'What time does our train leave tomorrow?' asked Mrs Torridge.

'Seven minutes past five in the evening,' replied Mrs Caldicot, who had their tickets in her handbag. 'We have to leave our rooms at the hotel by eleven in the morning. But they said that we can leave our luggage there. The hotel coach will be ready at three thirty to take us to the station. Because of the hour difference, we arrive back in London at half past six.'

'That's a long time to go without food if we run out of money,' Mrs Merivale pointed out. 'We'll need money for lunch and something for the train.'

'A long time without food,' agreed Mr Merivale who always trusted his wife's judgements and instincts, especially where food was concerned.

'And we'll definitely need some food for the train,' pointed out Mr Williams. 'We won't have Miss Nightingale's broken biscuit crumbs for the return journey.'

'They've just about all gone,' said Miss Nightingale glumly. Her broken biscuit crumbs, served straight from the pocket, had been a great success with everyone. No one had minded the bits of fluff that seemed to be an inevitable part of the package.

'Well, I suppose we could…,' began Mrs Caldicot. She then stopped, as though still thinking. She was, she realised, being a trifle naughty. She knew exactly what everyone in the room really wanted to do.

There was a pause, heavily pregnant with expectation.

'Could what?' asked Mr Livingstone, desperate for her to continue and to turn the rest of the thought into words.

Everyone in the room was looking at Mrs Caldicot and everyone was waiting for her to finish her unspoken thought. Everyone thought they knew what she was going to say. Everyone knew what they wanted her to say. Everyone wanted to say it but didn't quite have the courage.

'…I suppose we could play some more music this afternoon,' finished Mrs Caldicot.

No suggestion could have been better received.

There was a good deal of smiling and cheering and several people (notably Mr Hewitt and Mr Roxdale) banged the table with their spoons.

'Those two are getting rather rumbustious!' whispered Mrs Roberts to Mrs Caldicot, nodding in the direction of Mr Hewitt and Mr Roxdale.

'I'm beginning to think of them as the terrible twins,' Mrs Caldicot whispered back.

All that remained was to decide where they should play.

And they voted unanimously to return to the Place des Vosges, undoubtedly the scene of their greatest success.

'We might not be able to find a space,' warned Jean-Jacques. 'The Place des Vosges is very popular with buskers and we are a big band. We need a lot of room.'

Mrs Torridge, Mrs Peterborough and Miss Nightingale were again excited to hear themselves described as being part of a 'band'.

'Oh, don't you worry, we'll find somewhere to play,' said Mr Livingstone with confidence born of a formidable combination of ignorance and faith.

And they did.

They played for another two hours, and pretty well filled Mr Livingstone's banjo case twice more. Their performance was, once again, a huge success, though at one point they had a slight scare when a policeman stopped and watched them for a while.

'Do you think he's going to arrest us all?' Mrs Caldicot asked Mrs Roberts.

'I don't care,' said Mrs Roberts with more courage than she would have ever thought she had. 'We can cope with anything they can throw at us.' Their success in raising money through the band had done wonders for her self-esteem.

But the policeman didn't arrest them.

On the contrary, he joined in singing 'I Do Like to Be Beside the Seaside', laughed a good deal and clapped heartily when the song finished.

Mr Livingstone did notice, however, that the laughing policeman didn't throw any coins into the banjo case. Still, as Mr Hewitt pointed out, he didn't confiscate their earnings or arrest them either.

And then Jean-Jacques said very sadly that he had to go to work.

And everyone else reluctantly admitted that they were tired and would like to go back to the hotel for a wash and brush up before they found a restaurant for their evening meal.

'Would you like me to telephone the hotel to see if they can send the coach for us?' Mrs Caldicot asked the band.

'Certainly not!' said everyone, speaking as though one unit.

'We'll walk back!' said Mr Livingstone.

'I can manage,' said Mrs Torridge. 'And if I can manage then I suspect that everyone else can too.'

'It's quite a long way,' warned Mrs Caldicot.

'When I was a girl I once walked from Kendal to Ambleside,' said Mrs Torridge defiantly. 'They're both in the Lake District,' she added, just in case anyone didn't know.

'But I expect your knees were in better condition then,' said Mrs Caldicot.

'Same knees, same hips, same feet,' said Mrs Torridge firmly. 'And now I've got my walking frame to support me.'

And so they walked back to their hotel. They walked at a leisurely pace, stopping twice for coffee or tea and a chance to rest their feet and legs.

And on their way they bought a new suitcase for Miss Nightingale, whose original case had collapsed and died at St Pancras Station, and two small gifts for Jenkins, who had been left behind.

Chapter Twenty Five

'Odds bodkins!' cried Raphael when he saw them. 'What ho, old beans! May I crave a boon?'

'Crave away, dear fellow,' said Mr Hewitt. 'Damned please to see you, old boy!'

As always, Raphael, resplendent in his colourful uniform, looked desperately pleased with himself. To be honest, he always did look to be comfortably settled towards the top end of self-confident. He was not the sort of fellow to hide his light under a bushel, or anything else for that matter.

But now he seemed especially proud of his new English words. And his new skill seemed to have added to his sense of self-importance.

He touched the peak of his cap but managed to do it in such a way that it made him look as though he were a superior officer acknowledging the presence of a lowly squaddie.

Mr Hewitt couldn't quite understand how he'd managed it but he respected the talent it doubtless required.

'Do you need taxis or a coach for this evening? Shall I book a club or restaurant for you?' He lowered his voice. 'I have access to very private clubs.' He winked, in a wink, wink, nudge, nudge sort of way.

'No thanks, old bean,' replied Mr Hewitt, speaking for all of them. 'But your English is coming along very nicely, my dear old thing. Tally ho! All the best. Chin, chin. Cheerio.'

'Tally how!' replied Raphael.

'Cheerio!' said Mr Roxdale. 'Without you we would all be up a tree without a paddle.'

'Cheerio!' said Raphael. 'Without you I would be up a tree without a paddle? Yes?'

'Oh absolutely yes,' said Mr Hewitt.

Mrs Caldicot who had listened in some horror to all this, hurried indoors. 'You shouldn't tease him!' she said to Mr Roxdale and Mr Hewitt when they entered the hotel.

'Just helping him with his English!' said Mr Hewitt, innocently.

Mrs Caldicot couldn't stop herself from grinning.

An hour or so later the band (for that is now how they thought of themselves) ate dinner at the same restaurant where they'd eaten the previous evening.

'I can't remember when I had such fun!' said Mr Merivale, who was not a man to throw words about carelessly.

And it was unanimously agreed that this was a feeling shared by one and all.

Ruth spent much of the evening sending texts and photos to Denise. She missed Jean-Jacques but he had promised to meet her outside the hotel the following morning and she was, therefore, a very happy girl. She told Denise that Jean-Jacques had promised to write to her when she was back in England. 'He asked me to be his girlfriend,' she told her friend.

And an hour and a half after they had eaten, they were all safely tucked up in their beds wherein they slept like logs.

And every face in every bed bore a smile bordering on a grin.

Chapter Twenty Six

The following day, the last of their short holiday in Paris, went by far too quickly. The group hardly seemed to have finished their breakfast and packed their suitcases before they were on the Eurostar train racing back to London.

But there was time for a little more fun.

When their suitcases had been carefully stacked in the small store room which the hotel kept for the very purpose, Mrs Caldicot and the band stood in the hallway while they decided what to do with their final few hours.

'I've always hated the last day of the holidays,' said Mr Hewitt. 'When I was a boy I tried to pretend it wasn't happening. Once when I was a kid and my parents had packed up all our stuff, I ran off and hurried down to the beach so that we couldn't leave the seaside. I was six and I made my last sandcastle and decorated it with all my paper flags. My dad was furious because it took them an hour to find me and we had a long journey to get back home.'

Curiously, he seemed to remember this rather sad story with some affection.

'It feels as though we've been away for months,' said Mr Roxdale.

'Years,' said Mr Hewitt. 'Probably decades…'

'It was thanks to Mr Twist that we all had such a wonderful time!' said Mr Livingstone.

Mr Twist looked embarrassed. 'I feel really bad…' he began.

'No!' said Mr Merivale firmly. 'You mustn't feel bad about what happened. It was heaven sent! Without those confidence tricksters the band wouldn't have existed. Just think of the fun we would have missed.'

'You gave us all an experience we'll never forget,' said Mrs Roberts, who had never before had quite so much fun.

'Three cheers for Mr Twist!' cried Mr Livingstone.

They cheered Mr Twist and everyone meant it.

Mr Twist, blushing with embarrassment, acknowledged the cheers with a wave of his hand.

'We've got 314 euros left,' said Mrs Caldicot. It seemed a huge sum. 'We'll have lunch later, but what does everyone want to do with our last few hours?'

It was an unnecessary question.

It was not quite a rhetorical question (in that an answer really was being invited) but it was the sort of question to which there is only one answer. It was on a par with asking a bunch of children playing on the beach if they would like an ice cream.

And there were plenty of clues around.

Mr Livingstone was holding his flute. Mr Hewitt had his spoons in his right hand. Mr Roxdale had his comb, wrapped in a fresh piece of paper, in the top pocket of his jacket. Mrs Roberts was holding her bongo drums. A slightly tearful Ruth, who was constantly rushing to the door to see if she could see Jean-Jacques (who had promised to be there to say goodbye), was gripping her home-made maracas, those two pea-filled jam jars. Mrs Torridge, Mrs Peterborough and Miss Nightingale were wearing their red, white and blue bobble hats. The rest of the choir (Mr Williams, Mr Twist and the Merivales) could be heard clearing their throats just in case they were needed.

And Mrs Caldicot herself was gripping Mr Livingstone's banjo in its very useful case.

So, the children voted for ice creams and the band decided to hold its final Parisian concert; its last impromptu recital or, as Mr Livingstone put it: 'The farewell appearance of the band's first European tour'.

Chapter Twenty Seven

At the suggestion of Jean-Jacques, who had arrived as promised, they held their last concert in a small public park called the Square du Vert-Galant.

The park is reached from steps leading down from the Pont Neuf, the oldest bridge in existence, and one which connects the Left and Right banks, right in the middle of the city. What happens in the park can easily be seen from the bridge and from the quays on both sides of the river.

They performed the three songs which had already proved so successful for them but they also tried out four other songs which Mr Livingstone had remembered and written out: 'I'm Henry the Eighth', 'Any Old Iron', 'A Little of What You Fancy' and last, but definitely not least, 'I'll Show You Round Paree', a song made famous by the music hall star Vesta Tilley.

And, as they had done every other time they had performed, they delighted the crowds.

It was not the age of the performers, the novelty of their performance or the slightly uncertain nature of the playing of some members of the band which provoked so much interest and aroused such enthusiastic support. It was the passion and the excitement with which they performed.

At the end of their concert, Mrs Caldicot collected the money from the banjo case. She took from the takings the money she knew they would need for their lunch and gave the Merivales some notes and coins to buy food and drink for the train journey. She gave some of the rest to two elderly looking tramps who were sitting in the small park. They would, she knew, both spend it on wine. But, she reasoned, it wasn't her place to tell them how to ruin their lives. When they got back to the hotel, she gave the receptionist a good tip, gave the chef a 20 euro note as a thank you and handed the receptionist some money to share among the other members of the hotel staff.

And while they waited for the coach to arrive to take them to the Gare du Nord, she gave Raphael a modest tip. He hadn't done anything to earn it but she couldn't leave him out.

'Tally ho! The games afeet!' he said, with a convincing smile which showed a dazzling array of expensively capped teeth.

When the coach arrived, it brought with it a fresh party of British tourists. They were school children and their teachers. The children, in their mid-teens, looked excited. Six school-teachers accompanying them looked harassed and apprehensive.

'Odds bodkins!' cried Raphael, as the new visitors descended the coach steps. 'May I crave a boon?'

The teenagers stared at him, confused. The teachers backed away a little.

'I beg your pardon?' said a stout and stern-faced woman in her fifties. Mrs Caldicot thought she bore a startling resemblance to one of the stone statues found on Easter Island. The woman had grey, unkempt hair which looked as if it had been cut with a hedge trimmer and she wore pink framed spectacles which dangled on a chain around her neck. She carried a clipboard and a copy of *The Guardian* newspaper and was clearly the teacher in charge of the expedition.

'May I crave a boon?' repeated Raphael with great confidence.

'What is it? What are you saying? Do you work here?' demanded the school teacher in a tone which had been honed by years of quizzing sulky teenagers. She lifted up her spectacles and perched them on the end of her nose. When she'd done this, she examined him as though he were a laboratory specimen.

'What ho! I am your friendly, English-speaking doorman,' said Raphael unabashed and relentlessly cheerful. 'If you need taxis, restaurants or an introduction to a private club, all you have to do is to ask.' He beamed at her. 'I am your man!' He then winked. It was his way of showing that he was a man of the world and that no requirement was beyond his ability.

'No you're not my man!' snapped the school teacher, whose 'husband' was a 48-year-old, 14 stone, cigar-smoking, female social worker called Cyril.

The always angry school teacher ushered her party into the hotel and turned back to snap: 'Bring the bags in!'

'I do not do the bags!' protested Raphael to her back. But the school teacher either did not hear or she ignored him.

'Toodle pip, Raphael!' said Mr Hewitt, as he followed Mrs Torridge, Mrs Peterborough and Miss Nightingale and climbed up onto the now empty coach.

Mrs Torridge had Mr Torridge's ashes on her lap. She told Mrs Peterborough that he'd had a thoroughly good time and that she was pleased that she'd brought him.

Mrs Caldicot, felt sorry for the doorman, who was standing staring in bewilderment at the school party's several dozen large suitcases which had been abandoned and were strewn about on the pavement. She reached into her handbag and gave him another 20 euros or so in small change.

Raphael grinned at them all and pocketed the additional tip. He hadn't made much money out of Mrs Caldicot's party but he liked them nevertheless. And he realised, to his own surprise, that he would miss them.

Ruth was, of course, the last to climb aboard the coach. She was wearing her jeans, her jumper and her shapeless anorak. The blue dress, together with her memory of being a singer with the band, was now packed away in the small, rather expensive suitcase she had borrowed from Mrs Caldicot's husband. She and Jean-Jacques had cuddled until the last possible moment. As she climbed up the steps of the coach, she and her French beau continued to hold hands for as long as possible. There had been promises to write (emails and texts rather than old-fashioned mail, of course) and vows that they would meet again soon.

And then they were all on the coach, making their journey back to the railway station, back to Eurostar, back to London and back to Real Life.

And they were all, every one of them, filled with imperishable experiences or, as our good friend Dr Roget would doubtless have put it, replete with memorable impressions, packed with never to be forgotten evocations, stuffed with glorious recollections and bursting with immortal reminiscences.

'This trip to Paris has been a real joy,' sighed Mrs Peterborough, her eyes closed as she thought happily of their concert in the Places des Vosges.

'It's been a real joy,' agreed Miss Nightingale with a sigh.

'The most exciting month of my life,' said Mrs Torridge.

'We were only away for three days!' Mrs Caldicot pointed out.

'Were we, dear?' said Mrs Torridge. 'Goodness me. The time seemed to flash by very slowly. I would do it all again in a moment. Can we come back next week?'

'The dark hair changing to grey, that hath won neither laurel nor bay,' said Mr Hewitt.

'What's that?' asked Mr Livingstone.

'Christina Rossetti,' explained Mr Hewitt. 'Until this trip to Paris I had won neither laurel nor bay. But I feel I've come back from France a victor!'

'Hear, hear!' said Mr Livingstone, who honestly thought that he had never had so much fun. He felt good about the fact that his memories of Paris were now predominantly good and heart-warming ones. The sadness and the anger from the War were still there, of course. They would never go away. But they were now accompanied by some very good memories.

Chapter Twenty Eight

The rail journey was uneventful.

There had been huge queues for the customs and border posts at the Gare du Nord but no one had taken much interest in them or their luggage. The French border guards were too busy chatting to one another to take much notice of the travellers. Mrs Caldicot was enormously relieved. She'd been terrified that Mr Torridge might be confiscated and doomed to spend the rest of his afterlife in a French customs shed.

Mrs Caldicot had given the Merivales two handfuls of euros with which to buy sandwiches and drinks for the train. The Merivales had done their food shopping at a small delicatessen near to their hotel ('much cheaper and far better value than at the railway station' said Mrs Merivale who knew about these things) and they had purchased a massive picnic: baguettes filled with ham or cheese, pains au chocolat, croissants, scrumptious French pastries, bottles of water, half bottles of wine, paper napkins and cardboard cups.

They ate their picnic on the train.

As they left Calais, about to travel through the Channel Tunnel, Mr Livingstone suggested they sing 'I Do Like to Be Beside the Seaside' but no one was in the mood.

The only excitement when a mobile telephone made a 'pinging' noise and Ruth squealed with delight as she received her first message from Jean-Jacques. It came, of course, accompanied by a photograph and an electronic kiss.

And then they were back at St Pancras. The adventurers were back on English soil.

'Do you mind if I just pop in here for a moment,' said Mrs Roberts, indicating a branch of W.H.Smith the newsagent, as they passed through St Pancras railway station.

'No, of course not,' said Mrs Caldicot, assuming that Mrs Roberts wanted to buy something to read on the train. She and the rest of the party waited outside.

Two minutes later Mrs Roberts appeared, gleefully holding up a book of stamps.

'Now I can send off my postcards!' she cried with delight. She stuck the stamps on the postcards, found a post box and posted them.

The rest of the journey went without either alarums or excursions.

A small coach was booked and waiting for them at their local station.

And Mrs Caldicot was thrilled to see that Jenkins was patiently standing beside the coach to welcome them all back home.

Chapter Twenty Nine

'I missed you,' said Mrs Caldicot when they were back at Caldicot House. 'I missed you a lot.'

'I missed you too,' said Jenkins.

'Did you like your present?' she asked.

Everyone had clubbed together and bought Jenkins a pipe. Mr Livingstone had spotted it in a shop window as they'd walked back from the Place des Vosges.

'It was a real surprise,' said Jenkins tactfully. 'Do they know that I don't smoke?'

'Yes, they do,' said Mrs Caldicot. 'That's why they didn't buy you any tobacco.'

'That was a good idea.'

'I thought so,' agreed Mrs Caldicot. 'Mr Livingstone said he thought you might like to grip the pipe manfully between your teeth when giving one of your lectures.'

'I could certainly try that,' said Jenkins. He put the pipe between his teeth. It was a classic straight stemmed pipe with a large bowl and it looked very smart.

'You remind me of Monsieur Hulot,' said Mrs Caldicot.

Jenkins nodded his approval. He said something but with the pipe in his mouth it was difficult to hear precisely what he said.

'What was that?' laughed Mrs Caldicot. 'I couldn't tell what you said. It sounded like one of my texts.'

Jenkins took the pipe out of his mouth and struck a Tatiesque pose. 'I said I like Jacques Tati. He is one of my favourite film makers.'

'I bought you a small present too,' said Mrs Caldicot. She reached into her handbag and brought out a small pocket knife. 'It's a Laguiole knife,' she said. 'The man in the shop said they are the very best French penknives. He said hunters buy them for cleaning out their pipes and for gutting wild pigs.'

‘They are the very best knives,’ said Jenkins, putting down the pipe and accepting the knife. He examined it carefully, opening the single blade and gently caressing the wooden handle. ‘This is rather beautiful,’ he said. ‘Thank you. I shall definitely use it for cleaning out my new pipe and if I find myself in a position where I am required to gut a wild pig I shall be prepared and able.’

They cuddled and cooed for a while.

‘I haven’t got a present for you,’ he said.

‘You haven’t been away.’

‘I did do that lecture so I was away for the day.’

‘So you did. How did it go?’

‘It went very well thank you. But there weren’t any shops there. One of those reality television celebrities was selling his autobiography and a television chef was promoting his book on 101 things to do with leftovers but I didn’t think you would find either of the books particularly attractive as gifts. I could have probably negotiated a good discount but even so…and, besides, as soon as I’d given my lecture and earned my bread and butter I wanted to get back home as quickly as I could.’

‘To feed Kitty.’

‘Indeed. To feed Kitty,’ agreed Jenkins. ‘I may be wrong but it is my impression that she does not like being left alone for too long. When I got back she sulked for almost exactly an hour. She wouldn’t come near me. Then, when the hour of sulking was over, she wouldn’t leave my side. She sat on my lap as I worked on the first page of my novel. It’s going quite well, by the way. I think I should be ready to move onto page two by next Wednesday. So, how was Paris? Did you have a wonderful time? What did you do? Did you do all the usual things?’

‘Well, perhaps not all the usual things.’

‘You went up the Eiffel Tower, of course?’

‘Not exactly up it, no.’

‘But you saw it?’

‘From a distance. It’s hard to miss.’

‘Just from a distance?’

‘We were so busy. We meant to go and take a closer look but there just wasn’t time. There was so much to do.’

‘You went into the Louvre, of course? You saw the Mona Lisa? The Venus de Milo?’

‘Ah, no. We didn’t actually see either of those.’

‘You didn’t see the Mona Lisa?’

‘We didn’t go into the Louvre. But we went quite near to it several times.’

‘But you must have visited the church of Sacre Coeur and wandered round the Place du Tetre where all the artists gather?’

‘No, what with one thing and another we never did get right up into Montmartre.’ Mrs Caldicot paused for a moment. ‘But I’m pretty sure that one of the postcards which Mrs Roberts sent included a picture of Sacre Coeur. That’s the white one on top of a hill isn’t it? The one that looks like a wedding cake?’

‘I believe it is.’

‘It looked very nice on Mrs Roberts’ postcard. She sent you a postcard but you won’t get it for a day or two.’

‘Is the French postal service still a little hit or miss?’

‘I don’t know. She didn’t post her cards until we got back to London.’

‘She brought the cards back with her before posting them?’

‘Yes. She couldn’t find a shop selling stamps.’

‘Ah,’ said Jenkins, nodding. ‘Did you manage to see the cathedral of Notre Dame?’

‘No, I’m afraid we didn’t get to Notre Dame. That’s the one where the Hunchback wandered about on the roof, isn’t it?’

‘I believe so. It’s the Gothic one on the island in the middle of the Seine. Took them around two centuries to build, I seem to remember reading when I first visited. It has graceful flying buttresses and rather fine Rose windows widely regarded as awe-inspiring examples of stained glass craftsmanship.’

‘We missed that one, unfortunately. We’ll get to it another time perhaps.’

‘But I bet you all walked up and down the Champs-Élysées didn’t you? You couldn’t have missed the Champs-Élysées! Did someone buy a beret, a key ring with a small model of the Eiffel Tower attached to it and a black T-shirt with the word ‘Paris’ printed on the front in gold lettering?’

‘Well, not really,’ replied Mrs Caldicot. ‘We didn’t get as far as the Champs-Élysées, though we meant to. Oh, wait a moment, Mr Twist did buy a beret. A navy one. It was cloudy on the morning we went to the Place des Vosges and he said his head was cold. But the cloud dispersed and it was a lovely day. He put the beret in his pocket and I didn't see it again.'

'Ah, so you got to the Place des Vosges. Did you go into the Victor Hugo museum?'

'I'm afraid we missed that,' admitted Mrs Caldicot.

Jenkins looked at her, slightly puzzled. 'But you surely sat at a pavement café on the left bank and had deep, philosophical discussions about the meaning of life?'

Mrs Caldicot shook her head.

She realised with horror that they hadn't done the touristy things. Not one of them. 'To be honest with you, we didn't actually do any of the usual stuff,' she admitted, with some embarrassment. 'The time seemed to go by in a flash.'

Mr Jenkins was thoroughly puzzled. 'Why don't I take you out to dinner, and you can tell me all about it.'

'That would be lovely.'

'We could go to that Greek place you liked? Or try the Thai restaurant on Holdborrow Road. Or we could go to the Imperial hotel on the ring road. Or there's a new French restaurant opened just a couple of miles away. Maybe you would like to go there. They say it's very authentic. A review in the local paper said they had genuine French waiters and excellent French food.'

Mrs Caldicot thought carefully about these options then she sighed and tucked her arm into her husband's.

'Do you know what I really feel like?'

Chapter Thirty

They bought two portions of cod and chips, both with lots of vinegar and plenty of salt and Jenkins had mushy peas as a side dish. The man behind the counter said they were lucky because they didn't often receive any cod from their wholesaler.

They ate their meal al fresco, or en plein air as artists like to say when they are working outdoors, sitting on a bench in the park. The restaurant had provided them with little, wooden forks but although Jenkins used his for his mushy peas, they ate their chips and their fish with their fingers.

As they ate, Mrs Caldicot told Jenkins everything that had happened on their trip to Paris.

'It is my experience that people under the age of 60 look at a bunch of old folk and all they see is a bunch of old people,' said Mrs Caldicot when she'd finished telling her husband of their adventures. 'Those in their 40s and 50s are the most bigoted and prejudiced against the elderly. There is no respect and no understanding. People don't realise or care that older people have done things, seen things, experienced things and still have much to offer. And they have such resilience and strength. When I first met Mr Livingstone, Mrs Torridge and the others in the Twilight Years Rest Home, I saw a bunch of people who just seemed to sit around most of the day. They were drugged and mostly they just sat where they were put.'

'You rescued them,' Mr Jenkins reminded her.

They both concentrated on their cod and chips for a while. Mrs Caldicot found a collection of crunchy, battered bits hidden in a fold of her paper wrapping. She pounced on them.

'Not really,' said Mrs Caldicot, who had been thinking. 'Once they'd stopped taking their damned pills, they mostly rescued themselves.'

'Oh, I disagree,' said Mr Jenkins. 'I disagree very much. You gave them a loving environment and it's that environment which has enabled them to blossom.'

'While we were away, I discovered what a remarkable bunch they are,' said Mrs Caldicot. 'They've all done astonishing things with their lives. I feel quite ordinary and rather ashamed of myself. I spent most of my previous life ironing socks and underpants for Mr Caldicot.'

'Socks? You ironed socks?'

'Oh yes, he insisted on having his socks and underpants ironed. He even insisted that I iron his shoelaces. He always had those flat laces and he said they got creased after they'd been tied.'

Mr Jenkins screwed up the wrapping paper in which his chips had resided and tossed the resulting ball of paper into a waste bin beside their bench.

He sat in silence for a moment and then took his wife's hand. 'You've done the most astonishing thing,' he told her. 'You may not have done too much when you were ironing shoelaces but you have become a trusted, respected leader for a group of people who, above all else, needed a guide,' he reminded her. 'And without your leadership, your guidance and your encouragement, they would all still be sitting in Mr Hawksmoor's rest home staring into space.'

He took Mrs Caldicot's empty wrapper and screwed that into another ball. This time his shot bounced off the rim of the waste basket and ended up on the grass.

'There's no age limit on blossoming or acquiring greatness,' he said. He stood, picked up the screwed up paper and dropped it into the bin.

'I didn't lead them,' said Mrs Caldicot. 'Not really. They just sort of followed me.'

'You were an inspiration to them,' insisted her husband. 'That's what real leadership is. And remember, your story has inspired millions of older people to realise that they don't have to accept being bullied and patronised and drugged. You helped all those people understand that just because they are old they don't have to give up, lie down and wait for the undertaker to come and take them away.'

'But it wasn't me who led the way in Paris. It was Mr Twist who had the idea of forming a band. And Mr Livingstone who showed us what to do.'

'But remember that until you took him away from that awful bloody rest home, Mr Livingstone spent most of his days sleeping.

When he did wake up, he played a bloody silly cardboard keyboard because that bastard Hawksmoor kept the piano locked up. And until you gave him a home, Mr Twist was living in a cardboard box on a traffic island. You gave all those people renewed hope and opportunity.'

They sat in silence for a while.

'We did have great fun,' said Mrs Caldicot. 'I wish you'd seen Mrs Roberts playing the bongo drums. And Mr Hewitt was amazing with his soup spoons!' She laughed as she remembered their concert in the Place des Vosges.

'I wish I'd been there to see it,' said Jenkins.

But he knew, and he knew that his wife knew, that if he had been with them in Paris there would have probably been no band. He would have found a way to obtain some money to replace that which had been lost. He would have made a phone call and money would have been sent to a nearby bank.

They both knew that his not being able to go with them had been curiously serendipitous.

'Oo, I nearly forgot! You will be able to see us in action,' said Mrs Caldicot. 'Calvin and Josephine, the two Americans, said they'd send over a copy of Calvin's film when he's edited it. He took a huge amount of film. Josephine told me he had probably shot enough to make a TV documentary!'

'I look forward to seeing that very much,' said Jenkins. 'You did great things together. Do you think the band will play again?'

'Oh yes,' said Mrs Caldicot with a laugh. 'No one wanted to play or sing on the train but I have no doubt that the band will be back. We were all feeling a little sad, you know. And I think we'd had such a good time in Paris that we were all a bit frightened that things might fall flat if we tried to resurrect the band on the train.'

'It was too soon, perhaps?'

'Exactly. But I have no doubt that the band will be back! Mr Twist was heart-broken when he lost our money but it must have been the most serendipitous financial loss in history! Is that the word I want: serendipitous?'

'It certainly is,' said Jenkins.

They sat for a while in comfortable silence.

Two pigeons, attracted by small pieces of food on the floor, came close to their feet. One of the pigeons, braver than the other, attacked half a chip; pecking it, worrying it, shaking it to bits. A huge crow landed on the side of the rubbish basket and dragged out one of the wrappers. Small bits of food fell out. The crow pounced on them.

'You and I will go to Paris soon,' promised Jenkins. 'Just the two of us. We'll have a romantic weekend with a boat ride on the Seine, dinner in the restaurant on the Eiffel Tower, shopping on the Champs-Élysées.'

'I'd like that very much. It sounds wonderful!' murmured Mrs Caldicot.

'But we will do no gambling,' insisted Jenkins. 'We will walk past card sharps without a second look. And there will be no music, I'm afraid. I can't sing or play any musical instruments. I can't even whistle!'

'Definitely no gambling!' agreed Mrs Caldicot without even a moment's hesitation. 'But do you not think I should take Mr Livingstone's banjo – just in case we need to make a little money?'

'We will take spare travellers cheques hidden in my shoe. We will not be taking a banjo. There will be no bongo drums, no spoons, no combs with greaseproof paper folded round them and definitely, quite definitely, no jam jars filled with peas.'

'OK.'

They enjoyed more silence. A squirrel ran across the grass in front of them. It was a beautiful, calm evening

'Would you like coffee?' suggested Mr Jenkins.

'That would be marvellous.'

'There's a café still open about a quarter of a mile down the road.'

'Let's go home for coffee.'

They stood.

Jenkins picked up the wrapper which the crow had pulled out of the rubbish bin. He allowed what bits of food remained to fall onto the grass. He then screwed it up again and stuffed it back into the bin. He wiped his fingers on a tissue and added the tissue to the bin.

'What's your next adventure going to be?' he asked.

'Oh good heavens, I don't want any more adventures!' said Mrs Caldicot with a laugh. 'I'm strictly a home bird now.'

Jenkins smiled but said nothing. He knew his wife very well and he knew that the excitement of the trip to Paris had thrilled her.

Given a month or two at home she would, he thought, be yearning for a new challenge; a new adventure.

He took Mrs Caldicot by the hand. 'I do love you,' he told her. 'You're a wonder!'

'Don't be an old silly,' said Mrs Caldicot, squeezing his fingers because she loved it when he said nice things to her.

'I'm the luckiest girl in the world,' she thought to herself.

And they went home hand in hand to the sound of Mrs Caldicot quietly singing, 'I Do Like to Be Beside the Seaside'.

Notes from the author:
If you have enjoyed this book, I would be enormously grateful if you give the book a good rating on Amazon. A good review (however short) really does make a huge difference.
God willing, Mrs Caldicot will be back.
Vernon Coleman

This is the third novel about Mrs Caldicot. The first two are *Mrs Caldicot's Cabbage War* and *Mrs Caldicot's Knickerbocker Glory*.
For more information about books by Vernon Coleman please see his author page on Amazon or visit www.vernoncoleman.com where there are hundreds of free articles and no advertisements.

16434348R00111

Printed in Great Britain
by Amazon